THE BOBBSEY TWINS:
DR. FUNNYBONE'S
SECRET

"The ghost ship!"

The Bobbsey Twins: Dr. Funnybone's Secret

By

LAURA LEE HOPE

GROSSET & DUNLAP

A NATIONAL GENERAL COMPANY

Publishers   *New York*

The Bobbsey Twins: Dr. Funnybone's Secret

CONTENTS

THE BOBBSEY TWINS:
DR. FUNNYBONE'S
SECRET

CHAPTER I

Bouncing Beds

"I CAN'T WAIT to see Dr. Funnybone!" exclaimed six-year-old Flossie Bobbsey. "Wasn't he nice to ask us to spend our vacation at his house? I'm so glad he's our doctor!"

"And he has a secret for us to discover," said her blond twin, Freddie. "That'll be exciting!"

"We're going to have fun in Florida!" their twelve-year-old sister Nan declared. Her eyes sparkled as she looked out the window of the minibus at the tall palm trees.

Bert, who was Nan's dark-haired twin, glanced around at the other children. "Where's Danny?" he asked.

Joe Alvarez, their young driver, stopped whistling. "Somebody missing?" He grinned. "Can't be! Count noses. We should have ten, including me."

The next moment there was a loud BANG!

1

inside the bus. Startled, Joe let the wheel slip. The children screamed as the minibus swerved off the road, bounced into a wide ditch and stopped. Quickly Joe climbed out of his seat. "Anybody hurt?" he asked anxiously.

"I'm not," said Nan shakily. Bert and the tall, good-looking boy seated with him, Charlie Mason, declared that they were all right too.

"So am I," Nellie Parks spoke up. She was Nan's age and had long, dark blond hair.

But Flossie and her seatmate, Susie Larker, were crying.

"I bumped my knee," Flossie sobbed.

"So did I," cried Susie. She was six, too.

"Let's see." Joe examined their legs. "Nothing broken. You'll be all right. How about you boys?" he asked, looking at Freddie and the six-year-old next to him, Teddy Blake.

"We're okay," Teddy replied.

"What happened?" Freddie asked.

"That's what I'd like to know," said Joe grimly. "That bang came from inside the bus!"

Bert made his way to the back and looked over the top of the next to the last seat. "Okay, Danny," he said angrily. "Stand up."

A big, red-faced boy rose and scowled at them. He held a large piece of limp green rubber in one hand.

"Did you pop that balloon?" Bert asked.

"Of course he did," Charlie Mason answered. "That's why he was hiding."

"What happened?" Freddie asked.

"He used a safety pin," Teddy declared, looking over the back of the seat. "I see it on the floor."

Joe's sun-tanned face was grim with anger. "Do you realize what you did, Danny Rugg?" he asked. "You caused an accident!"

"It was just a joke," Danny mumbled.

"Well, it's not funny," Nellie burst out.

"We could have been badly hurt," Nan said hotly as she wiped away Flossie's tears.

"I'd like to give you a punch in the nose." Bert glared at Danny.

"Okay," Joe interrupted swiftly, "let's cool it. We must get this buggy back on the road. Everyone out!"

As the children climbed from the bus, an old gray sedan pulled to the side of the road behind them. Two young men and a girl jumped out.

"Anybody hurt?" the girl asked anxiously. The three newcomers wore blue jeans with long loose shirts. The girl and one of the young men were tall and had curly brown hair.

"We're okay," Joe replied. "Thanks."

The girl gave a sigh of relief. "I'm glad! We saw you go off the road."

The other young man was slender and handsome with a dark mustache. He had been looking over the children and the bus.

"Wow!" he exclaimed softly. "Nine kids! What is it? A baseball team?"

The children giggled.

Joe grinned. "No. These are the Bobbsey twins and their friends from the North. They've come to visit my boss."

Nan introduced the other children.

The man with the mustache said that the girl's name was Jean Tomson. "This is her brother Jon and I'm Gus Wilson."

"We're free-lance photographers," said Jon.

Freddie spoke up. "We've come to Florida to visit Dr. Funnybone."

"Dr. Funnybone!" said Jean. "I've heard of him. He writes books for children—he's famous!"

"He lives in Lakeport where we do," Bert said, "but he has a vacation house near here."

"His real name is William Carson," Nan explained. "Every year he writes a new book, and this year he decided to put in some children's stories and pictures."

Joe explained that the doctor had held a contest in Lakeport. The winners had been invited to come to Florida the day after Christmas and help work on the book.

"We flew down all by ourselves!" Susie piped up. "Our mommies and daddies put us on the airplane in Lakeport and Joe met us in Miami."

"Are you going to write a story, too?" Jean asked Danny, who was kicking one of the bus tires.

"Course not!" said Danny. "I wasn't in the contest. I wouldn't work on their old book for a million dollars!"

Joe explained that Danny was going to stay with an aunt while his parents went on a cruise.

"Her house is in Tavernier, not far from the doctor's," Joe added.

"We're neighbors then," said Jean. "We live in a trailer camp north of that town."

"You must know Dr. Carson's place," said Joe. "He owns that big estate on the bay and the island across from it."

The three photographers looked surprised. "You don't mean that old-style Florida house with the high-peaked roof?" Gus asked.

"That's it," said Joe.

"But the place is empty—it's been vacant for years."

"Right," Joe agreed. "The doctor has spent his winter vacations in Arizona for the past five years. But he arrived last night. My mother and I work for him whenever he uses the place."

"You can't stay there," said Jean. She sounded worried.

"Why not?" Nan asked.

"The island," Jon put in quickly, "the one called Silver Key—does he plan to use it?"

"Sure," Joe replied. "I guess these kids will be exploring there."

The three newcomers exchanged looks.

"Listen, I don't want to scare you," said Jon,

"but you'd better keep away from that island. People have seen strange things there lately."

"What do you mean?" Nan asked.

"They say it's haunted by Spanish ghosts. And a phantom ship has been seen near it."

"It sounds like a great mystery!" Bert spoke up, his eyes sparkling. "Tell us more."

"About four hundred years ago," Jon began, "Spain sent fleets of ships to Mexico for gold and silver. One galleon was wrecked on the way home and pieces of it were washed up on the island. There's a legend that the captain, his wife and the first mate haunt the key looking for something that was hidden in the ship. The woman sings a sad song as she searches."

"Have you seen the spooks, Joe?" asked Flossie.

The young man looked uncomfortable. "No. But Dr. Funnybone and I did see the galleon last night. It was weird."

"You don't believe in ghosts, do you?" asked Nellie.

"No," he replied, "but something very odd is going on."

"We love to solve mysteries," said Nan. "And now we have two—this one and Dr. Funnybone's secret!"

"The detective work will have to wait," said Joe. "Let's get this buggy back on the road."

Jon got a heavy rope from his car and soon the men and older boys had the minibus out of the ditch. Fortunately it was not damaged. Everyone except Danny thanked the photographers for their help.

"That's all right," said Gus as the three climbed back into their own car. "Just take our advice and forget about Silver Key!"

"Why do they call the island a key?" asked Teddy when their rescuers had driven off.

"Key is the English word for *cayo* which means island in Spanish," Joe explained. "Because the Spaniards settled Florida some of their words are still used here."

"We're on Key Largo now," said Bert as the bus hummed down the highway. "It's the largest of the string of islands off the southern tip of Florida."

"Right," Joe added, "and this highway connects them."

It was dark when the minibus reached the small town of Tavernier. Joe stopped in front of a pink stucco house. A thin, smiling woman in a blue pants suit hurried out to greet them. Joe unstrapped Danny's bag from the roof of the bus and carried it onto the porch. Mrs. Rugg thanked him for bringing her nephew, but Danny clumped into the house without a word.

The minibus went off. Ten minutes later it pulled onto a side road and turned into a winding driveway lined with high, thick bushes. At the end stood a large lighted house. As they stopped in front, a tall, broad-shouldered man with white hair and a short beard hurried out to the car.

"Hello, everybody!" he boomed.

"Dr. Funnybone!" cried Flossie. The children piled out and clustered around him for hugging and handshaking.

"Come into the house," he said warmly. "I'm glad you're here."

As the children trooped onto the long screened porch a short, stout woman in a pink dress came out. Her black hair was wound around her head in a thick braid.

"Oh, so many nice children!" she said happily and hugged all the little ones.

"This is Mrs. Alvarez, my housekeeper," said the doctor. "She'll take good care of you."

"That's my mother," called Joe, who was unloading bags from the bus. "She's a great cook!"

Joe's mother beamed as the doctor introduced each child. "You call me Mama Luisa," she said.

The girls followed her into a cool hallway. When the boys, Joe and the doctor had brought in the luggage, the travelers told about the bus accident.

"I was afraid Danny would make trouble," said the doctor, frowning. "I'm glad no one was hurt."

He suggested that the tired children go to bed at once. Mama Luisa led them up the wide staircase. At the top the housekeeper pointed to a door on the right and said, "Boys in there." Then she opened the next door and said, "In here—the girls."

In the middle of the large room stood two big, low beds. One was covered with a blue spread, the other red. Each spread had a golden sun in the middle.

"They look so great!" exclaimed Nan and plopped down on the blue one. She gave a little screech as the mattress sank and then billowed up around her.

At the same time yells and laughter burst out next door.

"The boys have funny beds, too," said Mama Luisa, grinning.

The next moment the girls were bouncing on them and giggling. Dr. Funnybone and Joe appeared in the doorway. "How do you like the water beds?" Joe asked.

"They're fun!" said Flossie breathlessly.

Dr. Funnybone said, "The mattresses are heavy plastic filled with water. They move whenever your body moves. Very comfortable!" He chuckled. "This house is full of surprises. Now good night, girls—sleep well."

Before long there was quiet in both rooms. All the children but Bert were asleep. He was too excited thinking about the two mysteries. Quietly he got up and went to the window. Below him was a large open yard surrounded by trees and heavy bushes.

On one side was a swimming pool. On the other was a little summerhouse. Beyond lay the big moonlit bay with a low island in the distance. For a long time he watched for the ghost ship, but nothing appeared.

Then he heard a woman's voice singing in Spanish! The next moment a figure in a long black dress and a lace scarf over her head slipped from the summerhouse and vanished into the woods!

CHAPTER II

Mr. Click

"It's one of the Spanish ghosts," thought Bert. He was still puzzling over the strange prowler when he went to sleep.

In the morning Bert was awake before anyone else. Quietly he dressed and slipped out into the hall. He knocked softly three times on the girls' door. It was a signal he and Nan used.

Moments later she looked out sleepily. "Come on, get dressed," he said. "We have work to do."

In a few minutes she came out in pink shorts and top. As they hurried downstairs Bert told her about the Spanish singer.

"What can she want here?" Nan wondered.

The twins went quietly down the front hall and found themselves in a large kitchen with a shiny red tile floor. A huge old-fashioned black stove stood in one corner. Nobody was around.

The children opened the back door and

stepped onto a long, screened porch. A big iron bell hung outside by the stoop. They hurried across the yard to a small house made of wooden lattices with a peaked roof. Blue morning glories grew over it.

Cautiously the twins went up two steps and walked inside. In the gloom they could see a seat which ran all the way around the little house.

"Look!" Bert picked up a large wilted pink flower from the floor.

"I'll bet the woman dropped it," said Nan.

The twins looked around carefully but saw no other sign of the mysterious visitor.

"Let's see if we can find where these flowers grow," Nan suggested. "Maybe there'll be another clue."

The children walked around the main house and down the drive to the road. They saw many flowering bushes but no blossoms like the one they had found.

"I love the doctor's house and the screened porches on all four sides," said Nan.

They stopped to admire the big swimming pool. It was surrounded by a stone patio with umbrella tables and chairs.

A moment later the bell loudly clanged twice. Bert and Nan ran past the swimming pool to the back porch.

Mama Luisa was there in a bright yellow dress.

"That's the breakfast signal," she said with a

smile. She led the way into the kitchen where the delicious aroma of frying bacon filled the air. The big round table was set for ten with a slice of yellow melon at each place.

"Oh, it looks so pretty!" said Nellie as she came in from the hall. The other children streamed in laughing and talking. The doctor came last with Teddy on his shoulder.

"May we ring the bell sometimes, Mama Luisa?" asked Flossie as they took seats.

"Sure," she replied. "Everybody takes turns. It is two rings for meals."

"And if there is an emergency we ring the bell lots of times, fast," said the doctor. "That means, 'Come quickly wherever you are!' "

While they were eating, Susie asked where Joe was. "He'll be here soon," Mama Luisa replied. "He sleeps at our house in Tavernier."

She set a dish of shining green marmalade on the table.

Flossie tried some. "Ummm, this is yummy! What flavor is it?"

"Lime," said the housekeeper. "We grow lots of them in Florida."

"Where do these grow?" Nan asked and held up the flower from the summerhouse.

"That's a hibiscus blossom," said Dr. Funnybone. "But there are none on this property. Where did you get it?"

Bert told about the singing woman and their

search of the summerhouse. The doctor frowned.

"I know that you've heard there's something strange going on around here. Joe said that the three young people who helped you out of the ditch mentioned the Spanish spooks."

"Is this mystery your secret?" Nellie asked.

"No, I know no more about this than you do," the doctor replied.

"We saw the phantom ship," said Mama Luisa, "and now a ghost has come to our gazebo!"

The smaller children looked puzzled.

"That's another name for a summerhouse," explained Nan.

"It can't be a real ghost," said Charlie Mason.

"True," said Mama Luisa, "but all the same it is very odd."

"Our mysterious visitor," said the doctor, "could have got the flower almost anywhere but here. I'm writing a book on wild plants and herbs, so I know everything that grows in this area—and there are no hibiscus bushes."

"She must have come from some distance then," said Bert.

"We'll keep our eyes open and try to catch her," the doctor said. "I'd like to know what it's all about."

"The Bobbseys are good detectives," said Charlie. "They'll find out and we'll all help them."

The girls struggled to make
the bouncing beds.

"When are you going to tell us your secret, Dr. Funnybone?" Susie asked.

The doctor grinned. "That secret is for me to know and you to find out!"

The children laughed. "Give us a clue," begged Freddie.

"Just keep your eyes open," the doctor replied. Suddenly he looked at his wrist watch. "All right!" he said crisply. "You have exactly ten minutes to make your beds and get ready to work on your stories. We'll meet on the side porch outside my study. Turn right at the foot of the steps. Now go! Shoo!"

The children raced upstairs and for a while the hall rang with whoops of laughter as they struggled to make the bouncing beds.

"We're done!" cried Freddie as he and Teddy drew the yellow spread over their bed.

"Come on, let's play racer!" said Teddy. He took four little toy cars from his suitcase and sat on the floor.

"They won't run on this carpet," said Freddie. "Let's take 'em down on the porch!"

The little boys scampered downstairs and the other children followed. They crossed a large room lined with books and went out onto the porch. The doctor was waiting with paper and pencils at a long picnic table.

"All right," he said, "let's get started."

As the children took seats on the benches,

Teddy put his racing cars on the floor behind him. "We'll play later," he thought.

"Now," said the doctor, "we must choose our subjects." He reminded the children that the stories for the book were to be about Florida. "We'll also need lots of drawings."

"I'm going to write about the mystery," said Bert. The older girls and Charlie liked the idea, and thought they would do that, too.

"And we'll draw pictures of palm trees and things," said Flossie.

The doctor nodded. "Fine," he said. "Now everyone be very quiet, please."

The children looked puzzled, but sat silent for a moment. Then Nan said, "What's that clicking noise?"

The others heard it too.

"Is it your secret?" Teddy asked excitedly.

The doctor smiled and said no.

"It can't be a clock," said Nellie, " 'cause there is none out here."

Bert frowned. "Anyway it clicks, not ticks."

Nan opened a small cabinet beside the door to the study. "It's not in there," she said. "That's all supplies. Crayons, paper, magazines."

Flossie was looking on the floor under the table. Suddenly she gave a loud sneeze.

"Bless you!" said the other children.

"ACHOO!" Flossie sneezed helplessly again and again.

"Stand up," said the doctor. "Maybe it's dusty under there."

Meanwhile Susie crawled under the table to look in a wastebasket.

"Oh!" she cried. "Here it is!" She pulled out the basket.

As the other children crowded around, Bert reached in and took out a small ball of grayish brown feathers. Two bright dark eyes stared angrily and a tiny beak snapped open and shut.

"An owl!" the children chorused.

"A baby barn owl," said the doctor with a smile. "I found him in my yard last month. He's tame."

"What's his name?" asked Flossie as the doctor placed the bird on his shoulder.

"Mr. Click."

"Why doesn't he hoot?" Susie wanted to know.

"He's too young," the doctor replied. "He really should be sleeping now. Owls sleep in the daytime, but I disturbed him when I was getting the pencils and paper out. He flapped around and fell in the wastebasket, so I decided to let him stay there a few minutes."

"He's just darling," said Flossie and gave a mighty sneeze. The owl flew up, but the doctor caught him. He put him on a wooden bird stand in the middle of the porch. "We'd better let him sleep now," he said.

"We saw a baby owl once before," said Bert, "when we were working on our *Rainbow Valley Mystery*."

"But we had to give it to the zoo right away," Freddie reminded him. "This one we can pet."

"I 'member that owl," Flossie murmured, starting to draw a palm tree. "His name was Hooty."

"We had a parakeet once," Teddy said. "His name was Bobby and he could talk."

"I'm going to draw a parakeet," Susie cried.

"No, I'm going to draw a parakeet," said Teddy. "You can draw a palm tree."

"Flossie's drawing a palm tree," Susie objected.

"Now wait a minute," Bert spoke up. "Are you kids going to talk all the time you're drawing?"

"We need quiet," said Nan, "so we can think up our stories."

"That's right," Dr. Funnybone said. "You four writers come down to the other end of the porch. I have a separate table for you with a box of paper and a typewriter."

"That's great!" said Charlie. "Let's go!"

"Enjoy yourselves," said the doctor. "I'll see you at lunch." He disappeared into the house.

After a while Freddie said, "We need crayons."

He went to the supply cabinet and took out a

large open box of loose crayons. The next moment he gave a yell, jumped aside and landed on one of Teddy's cars.

"Yow!" Freddie went flying backward and fell under a shower of crayons!

CHAPTER III

Spilling the Beans

"FREDDIE!" FLOSSIE CRIED. "Are you hurt?"

The little boy took a deep breath. "I—I guess not," he said. "I just sat down hard, that's all."

The older children hurried over from the other end of the porch.

"What happened?" Nan asked as she helped Freddie to his feet.

"A mouse ran out of the cabinet," Freddie replied.

"So what?" asked Charlie. "You've seen mice before."

"Yes, but this was a blue mouse."

"A what?" the others cried.

"A blue mouse," Freddie repeated. "I know it sounds crazy, but I really saw it."

Bert laughed. "Come on now, Freddie. You know we're not going to believe that."

The little girls giggled. "A blue mouse!" said Flossie. "You're funny, Freddie."

"I'm not being funny. I saw it."

Nan smiled. "Maybe you should draw one for the book. We'll have a section called, 'Wild Animals I Saw in Florida.' "

Freddie's face grew pink. "I'm not fooling!" he insisted.

"Yeah, yeah," said Charlie cheerfully. "Now everybody back to work."

The four writers returned to their table.

"I'm going to have a pirate ship in my story," Charlie announced.

"And have it capture a Spanish galleon," Bert said.

"With a beautiful lady on it!" Nellie said and Nan giggled.

Charlie made a face, then all of them got to work.

The younger children drew quietly. Now and then Freddie would glance at the cabinet and shake his head, puzzled.

About five minutes before noon Mama Luisa appeared in the doorway of the doctor's study. "Psst!" she said loudly and beckoned to Flossie.

The little girl followed her into the house. "You can ring the lunch bell," said the housekeeper.

At the sound of the two loud clangs, the children hurried to wash their hands, then trooped to the dining room. The doctor was waiting at the head of a long table covered with a white cloth.

As they took seats Mama Luisa brought out platters of chicken sandwiches, then a big bowl of something golden brown.

"Fried bananas," she explained. "We have lots of nice bananas in Florida."

"They're delicious," said Nellie as she tasted the hot, sweet dish.

"They're yummy!" Flossie agreed.

"Do you like 'em more than lime marmalade?" asked Freddie.

"I don't know," she said. "They're both good!"

"You can have them every day," said Mama Luisa as she put a dish of marmalade near Flossie.

"Are we going to work on the book now?" asked Charlie when they had finished lunch.

"No," said the doctor. "Half a day is enough. This afternoon you can play in the pool if you like. But first we take a little siesta after lunch. That's Spanish for a nap. It's the custom in hot places, you know."

"A siesta will be fun here," Susie piped up, " 'cause we just love our bouncy beds!"

An hour later the children raced outside in bathing suits. When they reached the pool, Bert kicked off his sandals. "Last one in is a lazy

"Last one in is a lazy lion!"
Bert yelled.

lion!" he yelled and jumped in with a splash.

"No, no!" cried Teddy. "Last one in is a blue mouse!" With a squeal he plunged in ahead of Freddie.

Yells and laughter and splashing filled the air as the children leaped into the cool, sparkling water.

Just then Joe came out of the house in his bathing trunks. "I'm your lifeguard," he called and bounded onto the diving board. He gave several high jumps, somersaulted in the air and hit the water in a smooth dive.

As he came up, the children clapped. "Oh, do it again, Joe!" called the girls and the boys begged him to teach them.

He worked with all the visitors for a while and each one learned a lot about diving. Bert was even able to do a somersault.

About three o'clock Dr. Funnybone came out to the patio in his bathing trunks. He was carrying a notebook, a basket of green plants and something large and flat wrapped in plastic. He put the articles on a table, then threw the package into the pool.

"There you go!" he called. "Dive for it!"

Bert took a deep breath, plunged and brought it up. He swam to the shallow end and the others clustered around as he opened the parcel. Inside was a large piece of white rubber.

"Blow it up!" Teddy urged. "It's a water toy!"

Bert began blowing into a nozzle and soon a huge white swan with big blue eyes took shape.

"We can ride it!" exclaimed Freddie.

"This is great, Dr. Funnybone!" called Nan. "Thank you!"

The other children thanked him, too. The doctor grinned and sat down in his lounge chair. He began to examine the plants and write in the notebook. Later, when the children came out to rest, Nellie asked what he was doing.

"I'm interested in the herbs and plants the Indians used for medicine and food. I think some of them might be very useful nowadays."

"What's this?" asked Bert, pointing to a clump of fern-like leaves.

"That's a *coontie* plant," he replied. "Our Florida Indians—the Seminoles—cook it to make *sofkee*—a kind of mush."

Flossie wrinkled her nose. "I'd rather have lime marmalade."

"I'm getting hungry," said Freddie. "What time is it?"

"Nearly suppertime," the doctor answered. "Why don't we all take showers and then come back here?"

"Here?" Freddie asked. "What for?"

The doctor laughed. "I'll give you twenty minutes—then come back and find out!"

When the boys came downstairs in fresh shorts and shirts they found Joe making a fire in the outdoor grill. Mama Luisa was placing platters of raw hamburgers on a large table next to it. Bowls of potato salad and hot string beans were already there.

By the time the girls came out, the meat was sizzling. Soon the doctor joined them. Everyone took a paper plate and helped himself.

After finishing, the girls cleared the plates and helped serve slices of ice cream roll while the older boys put out the fire.

As it started to get dark, the doctor switched on low yellow lamps at the corners of the terrace.

"These keep the bugs away," he explained.

"May we take a walk along the bay, Dr. Funnybone?" Bert asked.

"If Joe goes with you," he replied.

"Okay," Joe agreed. "But you'll need sweaters."

"I'll get them," said Nan.

"I'll help," Flossie offered.

As the sisters went through the kitchen, they saw that Mama Luisa had already tidied up and gone. They could hear the television in her room.

On a stool by the sink was a bushel basket. Nan peeked into it.

"More string beans," she said. "Oodles of 'em!"

The girls hurried through the dim hall and went to their room. Nan picked up Nellie's sweater and her own.

"I'll get the boys' things," she said and went out.

Flossie found her own pullover and Susie's. As she stepped into the hall, the little girl stopped and gasped. In the gloom she saw a mouse run down the stairs. It was pink!

"Nan! Nan!" cried Flossie. "Come here!" At the same time she dashed after the creature, sweaters trailing.

She saw the tiny mouse zip down the main hall and raced after it. Running into the kitchen, she tripped over a sweater sleeve and fell against the stool. Down came the bushel basket! Hundreds of beans spilled over Flossie!

As she began to cry, Nan ran in from the hall. "What happened!" she exclaimed.

A door beside the stove burst open and Mama Luisa rushed out.

"What's wrong? Who's hurt?" she cried.

She was wearing a red bathrobe and her hair hung down in a long, thick braid. "Oh, poor baby," she said and knelt beside Flossie.

Meanwhile Nan had found the light switch and flicked it. Just then Dr. Funnybone hurried up to the girls from the hall. The others crowded in from outside.

"I fell," sobbed Flossie, "and bumped my knee—the one I hurt on the bus!"

"I'm sure it's nothing serious," said the doctor, looking at the knee. "Just a bruise."

"You're full of beans," said Freddie to his twin, trying not to laugh.

"Why were you running?" asked Nan.

"I was chasing a pink mouse," said Flossie.

Nellie chuckled. "Flossie has to be just like Freddie. If he sees a blue mouse, she has to see a pink one."

"I *did* see a pink one!" Flossie insisted.

"Sure you did," said Nan with a smile.

Bert remarked, "It was so dim in here, I don't think you can be sure what you saw."

Flossie's lip started to quiver again. "But I *did* . . ."

"Of course you did, little darling!" said Mama Luisa. She picked Flossie up and put an arm around the little girl. "Whatever you say, that's all right. Here, I'll fix you a little cracker with some lime marmalade. That'll make your knee better."

"She's right," said the doctor. "Then put on your sweater and take a walk with the others."

While Flossie ate the cracker, the other children picked up the beans and put them back into the basket.

"Cheer up, Flossie," said Bert with a grin. "You did a great job of spilling the beans!"

Despite herself Flossie giggled. Before long she was holding Nan's hand and walking happily down the winding path from the backyard to the beach.

At the bottom a boathouse and dock gleamed white in the moonlight. The group started along the sandy shore. Bert stopped and gazed across the bay at the low, dark shape of the island.

"Why do they call it Silver Key?" he asked Joe.

The young man shrugged. "I don't—"

He stopped with an exclamation and the others gasped. A full-rigged Spanish galleon had sailed out from behind the island!

"The ghost ship!" exclaimed Charlie.

CHAPTER IV

An Opty Loosion

THE TALL SHIP sailed around the island and vanished behind it. The children and Joe stared across the bay, unable to believe what they had seen.

"I don't understand it," said Joe. "There are no more Spanish galleons sailing the seas. Those ships have not been used for hundreds of years."

"And yet we saw one," said Nan.

"It was spooky." Flossie shivered.

Susie tugged Nellie's hand. "Let's go back to the house," she urged.

The children hurried up the sandy path between high bushes. They headed for the yellow lights gleaming on the patio. The doctor was standing beside his lounge chair looking toward the bay.

"You saw the ship, I guess," he said as they hurried over to him.

"Yes," Bert answered. "Where did it come from? What can it be?"

The doctor shook his head, puzzled. "I don't believe in ghosts or ghost ships," he said. "Maybe it's an optical illusion."

"What's an opty loosion?" asked Flossie.

"An optical illusion," he said, "is when you think you see something that isn't there—or when something isn't really the way it looks."

"Flossie's pink mouse was probably an optical illusion," said Nan.

"And Freddie's blue mouse," Teddy added.

Freddie looked doubtful. "Maybe it was, 'cept I *know* I saw the mouse, even if everybody knows there is no such thing!"

"Don't worry about it any more tonight, Freddie," said the doctor kindly. "We'd all better go to bed."

The children said good night and Joe turned out the patio lights. On the way upstairs Teddy yawned. "Freddie had a loppily-loosion!"

The little girls giggled. "No, he didn't!" said Flossie. "He had an opty-tick!"

"Loptystick and ticklety-ops," sang Freddie.

Flossie spoke up. "Who can say:

'Lopty-sticks and ticklety-ops,
Wickelty-snickelty peppermint drops?' "

"I can," said Susie. "I can say it real fast!" She tried but stumbled over the words. She giggled, then the small twins and Teddy began saying it as fast as they could. Amid much laughter they all went to their rooms.

The children were disappointed when they awoke the next morning. It was raining too hard for them to go outdoors. But the hours passed swiftly as they worked on their stories, played games and watched television.

At bedtime Nan and Nellie were rocking happily on their water mattress when Flossie came in with her bathrobe belt trailing.

"Susie's still brushing her teeth," she said and bounced onto her bed.

Moments later the door burst open. "I saw one!" Susie shrieked, waving her toothbrush. "A purple mouse! In the hall!"

Flossie hopped up and dashed out after Susie. The other girls grinned at one another.

"Come on," said Nan with a laugh. "We'd better see the purple mouse!"

When they stepped into the hall Teddy and Freddie were there, shouting for everyone to come out.

"An orange mouse!" Teddy cried. "It went down the stairs. I'll show you!"

"It was purple!" Susie insisted.

The little boys had already leaped on the banister. As they zipped down, the four older children looked after them.

"Oh, no!" cried Nan, and Nellie yelled, "Look out!"

Mama Luisa had just come to the foot of the

steps to see what was the matter. Flossie screeched and Susie covered her eyes as Teddy and Freddie flew off the banister right into the stout housekeeper.

"Oof!" she cried, staggered backward and fell into a big chair beside the front door. The boys tumbled at her feet.

As the other children raced down in their pajamas, Dr. Funnybone came running from the kitchen. He was still dressed in slacks and shirt.

"Is anybody hurt?" he asked anxiously.

Freddie looked sheepish. "I'm all right," he said.

"Me too," Teddy answered and stood up. "Mama Luisa got the worst of it."

The housekeeper took a deep breath and pushed herself out of the chair. "Nothing broken," she said. "What were you playing?"

"We were chasing an orange mouse," Teddy explained.

Mama Luisa looked at him in amusement. "Are you sure it was an orange mouse?"

"It was purple," Susie insisted.

The housekeeper shook her head. "Colored mice! Imagine!"

"From now on you children take it easy," said the doctor firmly. "We don't want any more accidents."

"We're sorry if we hurt you, Mama Luisa," said Freddie, and Teddy also apologized.

"Oof!" Mama Luisa cried.

"It's all right," she said gently. "But no more nonsense now. Everybody to bed!"

On the way up the stairs, Bert said to the younger children, "This mouse joke has gone far enough. If you keep it up somebody's going to get hurt."

"It's not a joke! I saw it!" Teddy insisted.

"Me, too," Susie said.

"And me, three," Flossie agreed.

"And me, four," Freddie chimed in.

The next day was a bright, clear Sunday. The doctor took the children to a nearby church. After lunch and a siesta the younger children were eager to play in the pool. But the others wanted to explore the island.

"Joe will take you over in my motorboat, the *Flying Lime*," the doctor said.

Teddy giggled. "I never knew limes could fly."

"Florida limes can," the doctor said teasingly.

The children hurried down to the dock where Joe was polishing the big, shiny craft.

"Hop aboard," he said when Bert explained where they wanted to go. "It's a beautiful day for a spin."

The twins and their friends settled themselves on the soft red leather seats. Joe swung down behind the wheel. With a roar they shot out across the blue-green water.

"This is not very deep," the young driver

shouted. "Sometimes you can see large fish quite plainly."

After a while he pointed off to the side of the boat. "There's a manta ray!"

"I see it!" Charlie exclaimed, as he spotted a large dark shadow in the water.

The ray was flat and its sides bulged out in points like wings. When the boat drew closer the ray swam away from it.

"The water around here is full of interesting creatures," said Joe. He cocked his head and frowned. "This motor's making a funny noise."

Nan was looking toward the island. As the boat drew closer, the children could see that the trees had thick roots and were covered by heavy, twisted vines.

"It's a mangrove jungle," said Joe.

"In some places the trees grow so close together you can't see through them," Bert observed.

"Right," Joe agreed. "We'll circle the island, though. Maybe we'll spot an inlet or cove where the ghost ship could be hidden."

They cruised slowly around the large island but saw no trace of the galleon.

"Let's land," Bert suggested. "We can explore better that way."

"Not now," Joe said. "The tide is low. If I pull in any closer the *Flying Lime* will go aground. We'll have to come back another time. Besides, I want to examine this motor."

"Look!" exclaimed Nan. She pointed across the water to a clump of bushes at the edge of the island. They were covered with beautiful pink blossoms.

"Hibiscus!" said Bert. "Like the one the singing spook left in the gazebo."

"Perhaps she lives on the island," Nellie suggested.

"We must come back soon," Nan said eagerly. "I can't wait to search it."

While the boat sped back to the mainland, the children watched the mysterious island grow smaller. What was the secret of Silver Key?

When they landed, Bert said, "You know, we haven't heard any more about Dr. Funnybone's secret. What do you think it can be?"

"At first I thought it was Mr. Click," said Charlie, "but the doctor said no."

"I'll bet Joe knows," Nellie said. "Do you, Joe?"

The young man smiled and shook his head. "I've known the doctor for a number of years. He has always had funny secrets to amuse people who visit him. But he has never let me in on them."

"We'll just have to keep our eyes open," Nan decided.

As they walked toward the house they could hear voices and splashing from the pool. Dr. Funnybone was in the water with the younger children, who were playing with the rubber swan.

"Oh, the water looks so cool!" Nellie exclaimed. "Let's go in!"

"We'd better work on our stories," said Nan. "We can go in swimming later."

The others agreed. As the young writers went toward their table, they passed the owl. He was asleep on his perch.

"Hi, Mr. Click," said Nan quietly. "Are you having a nice nap?"

One bright dark eye opened slowly and stared at her. *Click!* Nan chuckled. "Sorry. Go back to sleep." The owl ruffled his feathers and closed his eye again.

"He's so little and funny." Nellie stroked the drowsy bird.

For a while the little group worked quietly on their stories. Then the girls thought it was time to go take a dip.

As they went to put on suits, Bert said, "Let's go down and look at the *Flying Lime*."

"Okay," Charlie agreed.

The boys walked down the path toward the dock. Suddenly they stopped short and listened. Someone was moving on the other side of the high bushes.

"We should never have come here now," a man's voice whispered. "Suppose they catch us!"

"They're all swimming," said a second man

softly. "We can slip in and out quick as a wink."

"I wish we'd never hidden the thing here," said the first man.

"Don't worry about that. It's Skipper Zingo we have to look out for. He's been hanging around here."

"I know," said the other. "He wants those Mexican birds. I feel sorry for anyone who gets in his way. He's dangerous!"

CHAPTER V

A Mysterious Light

QUIETLY BERT LEFT the path and slipped between the bushes. As Charlie followed, he stepped on a stick. *Crack!* At the noise there was a muffled exclamation in the brush ahead and the sound of somebody crashing through the undergrowth.

"Come on!" Bert whispered. "After them!"

He darted forward but was suddenly pulled up short by sharp thorns. At the same moment Charlie was caught. They could not move either way.

When they finally pulled themselves loose, the men they had overheard were gone.

"They must have had a car near here or a boat," said Bert, "but I didn't hear a motor."

"Let's go down to the shore, anyway," said Charlie.

The boys ran to the dock. Joe was working on the motor of the boat.

"Hi!" he said. "What's up?"

The boys told him what had happened. Joe raised his eyebrows. "Sounds like you almost caught some of the spooks."

"We'd have had 'em, too," said Charlie, "but we got stuck in some thorny bushes."

He pulled several large flat pods from his dungarees and showed them to Joe.

"Yes. Those are the seed pods of the 'pull-and-haul-back' plant," said Joe. "The little spines on them can really hold you tight."

"What do you suppose the spooks have hidden here?" Bert pondered.

Joe shrugged. "Who can say? All I know is they didn't come by boat or I'd have seen them."

"They must have had a car," Charlie decided. "If they parked far away we wouldn't hear the motor."

"Joe, did you ever hear of Skipper Zingo?" Bert asked.

Joe shook his head. "But my cousin Carlo in Miami is a sponge fisherman. He knows almost every skipper in these waters. We'll go see him tomorrow if the doctor says okay."

"That would be great," said Bert. "What do you think the Mexican birds are?"

"I don't know, but there's a park called the Parrot Jungle on the way to Miami. Perhaps you could pick up a lead there."

The boys thanked him and hurried back to the pool. They reported their adventure to the others.

The doctor listened thoughtfully. "By all means you must go to Miami with Joe tomorrow. I already had intended to take you to the bird park and the Seaquarium there."

"What's the Seaquarium?" asked Freddie.

"It's a big park with a very large swimming pool for sea creatures. You'll see trained dolphins there."

"We could draw pictures of them for the doctor's book." Flossie clapped her hands.

For the rest of the afternoon the children played in the pool. Once Bert asked the doctor to give them a hint to his secret.

"Keep your eyes open!" was all the jolly man would say.

That evening when it was dark Dr. Funnybone asked his guests if they would like to feed Mr. Click.

"Oh, yes!" exclaimed Freddie. "What does he eat?"

"If he were living in the wild, he would catch mice and bugs," said the doctor, "but here he eats raw hamburger."

Flossie was sent to the kitchen to ask Mama Luisa for the meat. Soon she returned with some hamburger on a saucer and the children went to the porch. The doctor lit a lamp on the cabinet. The owl fluttered his feathers and turned his head to look at them.

"Good evening, Mr. Click," said Nan. "We'll be going to sleep soon, but you're just waking up!"

The owl opened its beak. The doctor popped a little hamburger into it. The bird swallowed and blinked its bright eyes.

"Oh, he likes hamburger," said Nellie.

Nan held up a bit of raw beef and the bird took it from her fingers. One by one, the others did the same. But when it came Flossie's turn she was sneezing so hard, the owl became frightened and flew off his perch.

"You sound as if you're getting a cold, Flossie," said Dr. Funnybone, "Let's take your temperature."

He led her into his study with her twin and Susie following.

The doctor took a thermometer from a case in a box on his desk and put it under Flossie's tongue.

"Oh, don't catch cold, Flossie," Susie begged. "If you do, you can't go swimming."

Flossie looked worried. "Oh womfulflump-humph," she said, shaking her head hard.

"Don't try to talk," said Freddie.

A minute later the doctor took out the thermometer.

"ACHOO!" Flossie burst out.

"You're all right," said the doctor. "You have no fever."

"Dr. Funnybone!" called Nan. "Please come here!"

He hurried to the porch with the little girls and Freddie at his heels. The other children were clustered at the far end near the gazebo.

"Look at the sky above the island!" Bert cried.

There was no moon and they could just make out the dark shape of Silver Key. There was a white glow in the sky above it.

"Someone must have a very bright light near the center of the island," said Bert.

The doctor nodded. "And the trees are so thick we can't see it. All we get is the reflection on the clouds above."

"Why would anyone want such a bright light on a deserted island?" Charlie asked.

"Maybe they're searching for treasure." Teddy giggled.

"I never heard of any on Silver Key," said the doctor. "But I'm not an old-timer around here. I've owned this property only ten years."

"Perhaps Joe or his cousin will know," Nan suggested. "Let's ask them."

"Let's go over to the key right now." Bert's eyes shone with excitement.

"Sorry, we can't," the doctor replied. "The boat has engine trouble. Joe said he'd have to pick up a part for it tomorrow."

The children were disappointed, but they kept watching the island all evening. Bert was still standing at his bedroom window around midnight when the light went out.

Next day everyone was up early. Soon the minibus was rolling along the main road toward Miami. The eight excited children sang and chattered as the miles whipped past. By mid-morning they reached the gates of the Parrot Jungle.

"Look!" exclaimed Freddie, and the other children cried out in amazement.

Perched in the trees and on benches were several large macaws. Some had scarlet feathers, others were blue and gold. All had long tails.

"Oh, they're bee-yoo-ti-ful!" Flossie cried.

Joe bought a package of sunflower seeds from a vending machine.

"You can feed the birds," he said, "but don't try to catch them or pull their tails. If they get frightened they might bite."

Freddie rolled his eyes. "And they've got big, strong beaks."

"You bet they have!" said Joe. "That's why there are signs around to warn you."

Nan held out a seed to a blue macaw seated on a bench. He cocked an eye at it, then leaned down and carefully took it from her fingers.

Bert asked an attendant if any of the birds came from Mexico.

"Yes," the man told him. "Many of them come from there. You'll see the same birds in Mexican drawings and carvings."

Bert thanked him and walked on. As the visitors strolled along the paths among the trees, Bert thought of something. Could the Mexican birds the men in the bushes had mentioned be part of an art treasure? He told Nan what he was thinking.

"The birds could be what they hid," she said.

"I don't think so," Bert replied. "They referred to it as a *thing* not *things*. But maybe they were looking for the art birds on the island with that bright light. Or it might have been Skipper Zingo over there!"

Their conversation was interrupted by Nellie. "Hurry, Nan," she called. "Come see the flamingoes dance!"

The older twins caught up to the others and watched a flock of tall, long-legged pink birds run across a lawn by a small lake.

"They're so graceful," said Nellie, "it's just as if they're dancing!"

The time flew by. It was almost noon when the children and Joe arrived back at the entrance. They stopped in a large open space where many of the huge, brilliant birds sat on high perches.

"We'll never have time to draw them all," said Flossie.

"Have your picture taken with them," said

the attendant, a middle-aged man with curly gray hair.

"Shall I, Nan?" said Flossie.

"Go on," her sister urged.

"Put out your arms," the man directed.

All the visitors watched smiling as the man carefully placed a blue bird on each of Flossie's arms and a red one on her head. Flossie grinned and the man took her picture.

Just then somebody yelled, "Boy, do you look silly!"

It was Danny Rugg! The boy dashed over and yanked the tail of one blue macaw.

The bird screeched and started to fly away. Its big claws caught on Flossie's blouse. As the bird flapped and squawked, she screamed in fright.

"Cut that out!" the attendant shouted at Danny. He and Joe swiftly disentangled the macaw. It quickly flew to its perch.

"What's the matter with you, young man?" the attendant said sternly to Danny. "Can't you read signs?"

"You ought to be ashamed," said Nan. "That bird might have bitten Flossie."

The boy grinned, took a gumdrop from a bag and stuck it in his mouth.

"He doesn't care," said Bert. "Danny's hopeless!"

Just then his aunt hurried over. "Oh, Danny, you're not in trouble again, are you?" she asked.

The bully yanked the macaw's tail.

"Yes, he is," said Joe grimly. "And we've had enough of his jokes."

Mrs. Rugg looked unhappy. "I'm really very sorry," she said. "Come on, Danny," she added sharply. "I'm taking you straight back to Tavernier."

Danny made a face and followed her toward the gate.

The attendant now gave Nan the Polaroid picture he had snapped of Flossie.

"That's great," said Freddie. "We can make our drawings from that."

A short time later the children arrived in Miami. After lunch Joe drove them across town to the Miami River. Here they parked on a side street among stucco buildings and walked to the waterfront.

It was lined with docks, and every kind of small craft was anchored there. The young twins spotted a white cat on the deck of one boat. They stepped close to the railing.

"Nice kitty," called Flossie.

At once they heard an angry voice inside the cabin. The door flew open and a thin, sharp-faced man strode out. He glared at the twins.

"Get away from here," he yelled, "or you'll be sorry!"

CHAPTER VI

The Sea Creatures

STARTLED, THE YOUNG twins backed away from the boat. The angry man stepped to the rail. "I won't have anybody spying around here."

"We just wanted to pet the kitty," Freddie told him.

Before the man could reply, a tall, brown-haired youth stepped from the cabin. It was Jon Tomson. His sister was with him.

"Leave the kids alone!" Jon said to the man. "They're not bothering you."

The thin man glared at them. "I'm warning you two," he said. "You'll do what I say or else!" He turned on his heel and disappeared into the cabin.

The Tomsons looked worried as they stepped up onto the dock. "What are you children doing here?" Jean asked, "and where are the others?"

Freddie explained that they had come to question Carlo, the sponge fisherman, about Skipper Zingo and the Mexican birds.

Flossie spoke up. "I hope that mean man on the boat isn't going to hurt you."

"We'll be careful," Jean assured her. "The trouble is, we rented a boat from him and now he wants more money than we agreed to pay."

"You'd better catch up with the others," said Jon. "Carlo's sponge boat is up ahead three docks."

"Don't hang around this boat," Jean warned.

The twins said good-by and ran along to a small dingy-looking craft. Joe and the other children were there with a short, swarthy man in a skivvy shirt.

"You must stay with the rest of us," Nan warned the young twins, "or you'll get lost."

Joe introduced them to the sponge fisherman.

"Happy to meet you," said Carlo, grinning. Joe spoke rapidly to his cousin in Spanish.

"I didn't know you could speak Spanish," said Freddie, surprised.

Joe smiled. "My family is from Cuba, but I was born here." He said that he had told Carlo about the island, the ghosts and Skipper Zingo.

"Zingo, Zingo," said Carlo and rolled his eyes upward. "No, I know no Zingo." He called something to two men in the boat. They were beating sponges with wooden paddles. The men looked up and shook their heads.

"What about the Mexican birds?" asked Bert.

"That I know," said Carlo with a smile. "They are supposed to be somewhere on Silver Key. The birds are made of silver. It's because of them that the island got its name. I heard the story as a child in Cuba."

He told the children that years before, a fleet of Spanish galleons had gone to Mexico for treasure. One of the captains had taken his wife along. While they were there she had bought two beautiful silver birds for her small son and daughter at home.

"On the way back they stopped in Cuba for supplies. The woman told a friend there that she did not trust the crew. She was afraid they would steal the silver birds, so she had hidden them in a safe place on the ship.

"Then the fleet was caught in a storm, and their ship sank. Parts of it were washed up on Silver Key. Legend says that the ghosts of the captain and his wife come back looking for the silver birds."

"I wonder where she hid them," said Nan.

Carlo shrugged. "Who knows?" Then he smiled and said, "Would you like to see us cut the sponges?" He led the way into a nearby warehouse.

In the center of the room sat four men with a pile of sponges. Each man had a long knife.

A young man with thick black eyebrows flicked the edge of his knife. "Very sharp," he said. "We need it that way to cut the sponges."

As the children watched, the men sliced the big brown masses into smaller chunks.

"That's how you buy them in the store," said Carlo. "We beat them first, so they are very soft when wet and excellent for cleaning things."

Freddie spoke up. "Carlo, who is that mean man in the boat with the cat?" He told what had happened.

"That's Skipper York," Carlo said. "He rents out boats. He's a tough one."

"He sounds as if he might be dangerous too," said Bert. "He could be Skipper Zingo except that he has the wrong name."

After thanking Carlo, the visitors walked back to Skipper York's dock. The boat was gone.

Joe stepped over to a neighboring craft where a man was polishing the brass rail. "Do you know where Skipper York is?" he asked.

The man pushed back his cap. "Who knows? He comes and goes and never talks to anybody."

The visitors walked back to the minibus. They drove across town to a large park with a big round building in the middle.

"This is the Seaquarium. Go on in and look around," said Joe. "I'll meet you here at the gate in an hour."

"Let's see the dolphins first," Teddy urged.

The others agreed and ran to the stadium. Upstairs they took seats overlooking a big pool. On one side was a high, railed platform. A young man in white trousers stood here holding a fish over the side. As he called, a huge dolphin, or porpoise, leaped from the water and took the fish from his hand.

Everyone applauded.

The announcer explained that the dolphins were very friendly creatures and were trained to do a number of tricks.

"I'd like a dolphin to play with," said Teddy.

Susie shivered. "They're awfully big. Maybe you could get a little one."

After the show the children went downstairs where they could look into the pool through glass windows. All kinds of fish, both beautiful and ugly, could be seen.

"There's a moray eel," said Bert. He pointed to a snake-like creature with a round, open mouth full of very sharp teeth.

"And a sawfish," said Nan as a fish with a long saw-like extension on its head swam past.

While they watched, a diver appeared in the tank carrying a bucket. He was well protected in a heavy suit and helmet. As he gave out food from the bucket, some of the fish in the tank hung back. Others like the dolphins and a giant grouper ate from his hand.

"This is a keen place," said Freddie. "What'll we do next?"

"Let's go on the skyride," Charlie suggested.

In five minutes the children were seated in a small capsule which ran on a cable above the park.

As they looked down at the wide lawns and flower beds, Flossie squealed. "There's Skipper York!" She pointed to a man hurrying toward the main building.

"As soon as we land, let's try to find him," said Bert. "I'd like to get a closer look at him."

When the ride was over, the children hurried toward the round building. Suddenly Freddie cried, "There he is!"

The skipper was sitting in the garden of the cafeteria. He was talking earnestly to a young man in dungarees.

"I wish we could hear what they're saying," said Bert. "If the other man calls him Skipper Zingo, we'll know we were right."

"We'll never get close enough to hear him," said Charlie. "If he yelled at Freddie and Flossie for spying, he won't let us go near him now."

Suddenly Nan noticed a red iron diving helmet suspended on a heavy wire from a pole near Skipper York's table. As she watched, a woman pulled it down over the head of her little boy and took a picture of him. Then she raised the helmet and they walked away.

"I have an idea," said Nan. "Freddie can put that on and get close. York will never know. Maybe he can hear what they're talking about."

While the other children watched from behind a large hibiscus bush, Nan and Freddie walked over to the diving helmet. Quickly Nan fitted the hood over her brother's head.

"Can you hear?" she asked. Through the helmet's glass front Nan saw Freddie shake his head.

Nan was discouraged, but she backed away and took several snaps. Skipper York scowled at them. Suddenly he stood up angrily and strode away from the table.

"Get out of my way!" he snapped at them and pushed Freddie aside.

The little boy stumbled and sat down with the helmet still on his head.

"You leave my brother alone!" Nan cried. She picked Freddie up, and removed the hood.

"That's enough, York!" said a deep voice. The man who had been at the table caught the skipper's arm. "Get out of here and don't come back!"

York jerked free and hurried off, muttering angrily.

The children thanked the young man. "That's okay," he said.

"Do you work here?" Bert asked the man.

"Yes. I'm a diver. I just got through feeding the fish in the big tank. My name's Jack."

"We saw you." Then Freddie asked eagerly, "Do the fish ever bite?"

"Sometimes the moray eel does. And the sawfish tries to saw me!"

"You're brave," Susie piped up.

"Maybe you can help us with a problem," said Bert. He explained that they were trying to

"You leave my brother alone!"
Nan cried.

locate Skipper Zingo. "We thought maybe Skipper York was Zingo."

"I don't know about that. He made an appointment to talk to me about a diving job. But he wouldn't say exactly where he wanted me to dive. I figured he was after treasure." The young man grinned. "Florida's full of treasure hunters."

"Did you say you'd do it?" Bert asked.

"No," Jack replied. "I didn't like his looks. There's something fishy about him."

Freddie chuckled. "But you like fish."

Jack laughed. "Not that kind."

The children thanked him again and started for the main gate. On the way they stopped in the gift shop. While the others selected postcards to send home, Teddy bought a large dried starfish. Outside, they told Joe what had happened.

"York's the kind of man to stay away from," he warned.

"And he's seen all of us now," said Nellie uneasily. "He'll be really mad if he meets us again."

As the minibus rolled along the highway toward Tavernier, Bert and Nan talked quietly about the mystery.

"I have a strong hunch that York is Zingo," said Bert. "Everything fits. He's a skipper, he's mean, and he's probably a treasure hunter."

"That's right," said Nan, "but the name is

wrong. Besides, Jack said there are lots of treasure hunters in Florida."

Bert nodded gloomily. "We're not making much progress on this mystery."

"Or on Dr. Funnybone's secret, either," said Nan. "What can it be?"

It was nearly dark when the travelers reached home. The doctor came out to greet them. He looked worried.

"I have bad news," he said. "Mr. Click is gone!"

CHAPTER VII

Midnight Beach Party

"GONE!" REPEATED NAN as the other children exclaimed in dismay. "You mean the owl flew away?"

"I don't know," said the doctor. He told them the bird had been asleep on its perch before lunch. "Afterward I took a siesta. When I woke up and came down, Mr. Click was gone."

Just then Mama Luisa appeared in the hall doorway. "It is no use," she said sadly. "We have looked all over the house. I think someone has stolen the little bird."

"Why do you say that?" Nan asked.

"Because when I was resting in my room after lunch I heard the front porch door open and then close. I thought it was the doctor. But now I'm sure it was the thief."

"But who would steal an owl?" said Nellie.

"Perhaps someone sneaked in to steal something else," Bert said, "and the owl woke up and flew out when the person left."

"We thought of that," the doctor replied, "but there's nothing missing from the house."

"I think we ought to search the yard," Nan proposed. "Mr. Click might be out there."

Everyone agreed and they split up into teams. Flossie trotted along behind Nan and Bert as they headed for the gazebo.

The three stepped quietly inside. It was gloomy, but they scanned the wooden lattice-work carefully. There was no small, dark bundle of feathers perched anywhere.

Flossie stooped and looked around the floor. "He's not down here either," she said. "ACHOO!"

"If you're going to start sneezing, you'd better go in the house," said Nan, "because you'll scare the owl away."

"I wouldn't want to do that," Flossie answered.

She went back to the house and soon the other searchers drifted in. No one had found any clues to the missing pet.

When it was time for bed, Susie asked uneasily if the spooks could get into the house again.

"I'll lock all the doors," said the doctor, "and we'll be perfectly safe."

"Do you think Mr. Click could find his way back here?" Susie asked.

"I doubt it," said the doctor sadly. He pointed out that the bird was very young and had never had to care for itself. "He's probably pretty scared."

Flossie went to the window and looked up into the dark trees. "Good night, Mr. Click," she called. "Don't be afraid. We'll find you."

"We hope," thought Bert as the children started upstairs for bed.

"Maybe Mr. Click is in the house after all," said Freddie. "Owls eat mice, you know. He might have chased that blue mouse and got lost somewhere inside."

"I wish you'd stop the nonsense about a blue mouse, Freddie," said his brother. "There is no such thing as a colored mouse."

"That's what you think," said Freddie firmly, as he went into the boys' bedroom.

"Yes," Teddy echoed loudly as he followed. "That's what *you* think!"

Flossie and Susie chimed in as they went into their room.

"It's funny," said Charlie. "They just won't give up that crazy idea."

When the lights had been out awhile, Nan got up, put on her robe and knocked on the boys' door. She used the special signal and Bert answered.

"I've been thinking," she said. "Freddie might be right about the owl being in the house. Let's search."

"Okay," her twin whispered. "I'll get my flashlight."

When Bert came out, he closed the door quietly behind him.

"Let's check the kitchen first," Nan suggested. "We can go down the back stairs."

The twins tiptoed to the end of the hall. Suddenly they heard a creaking noise in the corner near the top of the steps. Bert flashed his light there.

The twins froze in their tracks. They could not believe their eyes. There sat a green puppy with white polka-dots! The next moment it shot down the narrow staircase into the darkness.

"Did you see what I saw?" Bert asked.

"I just can't believe it!" whispered Nan. "A polka-dot dog and it seemed alive!"

"Come on!" Bert urged. "Let's see if we can find it!"

He hurried down the stairs with Nan at his heels. They stepped into the kitchen.

"Turn on the light," Nan whispered.

Bert made his way to the switch beside the doorway into the hall and stopped short. Had he seen a light under the door of the closet beneath the stairs? The next moment it was gone!

He turned on the kitchen light. There was no sign of the dog. Bert walked over and tried the handle to the hall closet.

"Locked," said Nan. "I wonder what's in there."

The twins stepped back into the kitchen where the housekeeper stood in her red bathrobe, blinking in the light. "Why are you out of bed?" she asked.

As Nan explained, Mama Luisa stepped over and put her hand on the girl's brow.

"No fever," she said and smiled. "So it must be more jokes. Green dogs?"

"Mama Luisa," said Bert earnestly, "we think Dr. Funnybone must know about these colored animals. Where is he?"

The housekeeper shrugged. "The doctor said he would look around outside one more time for the owl before going to bed. Or maybe he is in his study."

"Thank you," said Nan. "We'll look."

"Mama Luisa," said Bert, "what's in the stair closet?"

"Some of the doctor's things," she replied. "He keeps it locked."

Mama Luisa went into her room. The twins turned off the light. They walked down the hall and peered into the doctor's study. It was dark. They stepped outdoors to look for him. A few minutes later they stood near the gazebo gazing around the starlit yard.

"Dr. Funnybone!" Nan called softly. There was no answer.

As they moved closer to the gazebo, Bert clutched Nan's sleeve. "Listen!"

The twins could hear clicking!

The twins could hear clicking.

They stepped inside and flashed the light around. The noise was louder.

"It sounds as if it's coming from under the seat," said Nan.

As Bert beamed the light down, they saw two dark, glowing eyes behind the lattice.

"Mr. Click's in there!" exclaimed Nan.

She tested the lattice and found that part of it was loose. As she lifted out the broken panel, Bert reached inside and scooped up the wide-eyed bird.

"Ouch!" Bert cried. "Stop pecking me. I'm your friend."

"Look what I found," said Nan grimly. She held up a half-eaten gumdrop. "Now we know who kidnapped Mr. Click."

"We might have guessed it," said Bert in disgust. "Danny Rugg!"

Carrying the owl, Bert hurried to the house with Nan at his heels. There was a light now in the study.

"We found him!" exclaimed Bert as he burst in.

The doctor whirled in surprise. Then his face lit up. "Wonderful!" he exclaimed. "Where was he?"

As the doctor tenderly took the owl and held it against his chest Bert told about finding the bird in the gazebo. Nan added the evidence of the gumdrop.

"Danny needs to be taught a lesson," said the

doctor. Then he smiled. "Now we will get Mr. Click a snack of hamburger."

After the little owl had eaten hungrily, the twins and their host went to bed. The next morning the other children and the Alvarezes were happy to learn of the bird's rescue.

"I'd like to give that Danny Rugg a kick in the pants," said Teddy.

"Who wouldn't?" Charlie asked.

"Forget him," said Dr. Funnybone cheerfully. "Tonight is New Year's Eve. We will have a midnight beach party!"

The visitors cheered.

After breakfast, Bert and Nan called a meeting of the other children in the girls' bedroom.

"We want to apologize to the young twins and Susie and Teddy," said Nan. Then she told what she and Bert had seen the night before.

"It's true," Bert admitted. "There really are colored animals running around this place."

"I'm glad you saw one!" exclaimed Freddie, while his twin, Teddy and Susie clapped their hands.

"I'm sure the colored animals are Dr. Funnybone's secret," said Bert.

Charlie grinned. "And *we* have to find out how he works the trick."

Bert nodded. "I have a plan. If anybody sees an animal, call out loudly and the rest of us will go looking for the doctor. Maybe we'll catch him at it."

"I'd like to examine the place where we saw the puppy," said Nan.

She led the way down the hall and knelt to peer into the corner.

"I've found something!" she exclaimed. On the baseboard she had spotted two tiny hinges. "There's a little door here."

Nellie knelt beside her. "But there's no handle to open it."

"That must be where the animals come out," said Charlie.

Presently Nellie remarked, "We're making progress with the secret. Now let's make some progress on our stories."

The four older children worked on their plots. Nan decided that the beautiful lady in her story should hide the gold before the pirates could find it.

"And my galleon captain could trick the pirates into leaving the ship," Charlie suggested.

The day sped by and an hour before midnight the whole household trooped down to the beach. They gathered around a cookfire where Joe and Mama Luisa were grilling hot dogs.

Later, as they were toasting marshmallows, the doctor held up his hand.

"It's nearly midnight," he said, pointing to his watch. "Listen!" The next moment the iron bell at the house rang out over and over again.

"It's Joe," said the doctor, "ringing in the New Year!"

"Happy New Year!" cried everyone.

Mama Luisa beamed and hugged all the children. The doctor opened a big box and passed out paper hats and horns.

The girls began singing "Auld Lang Syne" and everyone joined in. Fifteen minutes later, the younger merrymakers were heading for bed, blowing their horns.

As the older boys helped Joe put out the fire, Bert pointed to the sky over the island.

"Look!" he said. "The bright light again!"

The doctor's face became stern. "We're going to get to the bottom of this mystery right now," he said. "You older children can come with Joe and me. We're going to the island!"

CHAPTER VIII

A Toy Clue

FIVE MINUTES LATER the motorboat was speeding toward the island. The sky above it still glowed with the white light.

"What can they be doing?" Bert wondered.

"It would be better if they used flashlights or a lantern so as not to attract attention," Nan said.

"We're in luck," Joe said. "The tide is high. I'll take the boat into one of the inlets." A moment later he added, "Okay, duck your heads."

He cut the motor and nosed the craft under some low-hanging vines into a narrow stream.

"The light is probably in the big clearing at the center of the island," said Joe softly as they left the boat. "I know the way."

"From now on," the doctor reminded them, "we must be very quiet. And no flashlights."

"Stay together," Joe whispered.

He set off with the children behind him and

the doctor bringing up the rear. As they moved along a rough path, the tangled growth was so thick that they had to hold the branches back for one another.

Suddenly Bert stumbled over a twisted root. The bough slipped from his hand, snapped back and hit Nan in the face.

"Oh!" she cried out in spite of herself.

"Nan, Nan, I'm sorry," he whispered. "I couldn't help it."

She bit her lip in pain. "I'm sorry I yelled."

"Shh!" said the doctor. "Wait!"

They listened for a while. Had any of the island prowlers heard Nan's cry?

At last the trekkers moved on. Then Joe raised his hand and they stopped again. Somewhere ahead a lantern moved among the trees and a woman was singing softly in Spanish. Both the sound and light were going away from them.

As quietly as possible they followed the singer and the lantern.

"She's heading off to the side," said Bert. "I'll bet she's trying to lure us away from that central clearing."

"Doesn't matter," Joe said firmly. "If we can catch her, we'll find out what their game is."

The six pursuers pushed onward. Suddenly Nan felt her feet sink into something wet and cold.

"Ugh!" she exclaimed. "We're in mud."

"The island is very swampy," the doctor said.

"We'd better get back to the boat!"
Joe warned.

Suddenly they emerged into a small clearing. All was silent. The lantern light was gone.

"She slipped away," said Joe.

Just then there was a sudden gust of wind and a rumble of thunder.

"A storm's coming," said the doctor.

The wind blew harder and the thunder cracked close at hand. The vines swayed and the branches lashed to and fro. As the four worked their way toward the shore, the wind blew harder.

"We'd better get back to the boat!" Joe warned.

"If it's torn loose from its anchor, we'll be stranded here!" the doctor shouted.

Clinging to one another, the six struggled along the path. Gradually, as they neared the shore, the storm quieted down.

Stumbling, breathless, out onto the narrow beach, the group stopped short in amazement. The moon was shining and the boat rocked gently on the quiet water.

"But—but this is impossible!" Bert exclaimed.

"How could it be storming in the center of the island and not out here?" Nan asked.

The doctor and Joe stared at the shimmering bay as if they could not believe it.

Nellie shivered. "This place sure is spooky!"

"There has to be some natural explanations for this," the doctor said, "but I must admit it has me stumped."

"Whatever it's all about," Bert pointed out, "the spooks kept us from finding out what they were doing with that light."

Speeding homeward in the boat, the children looked back at the island. The glow was gone from the sky.

"The spooks won this round," Charlie said. "But we'll come back!"

Next morning the breakfast bell did not ring until ten o'clock. When the children appeared in the kitchen Mama Luisa was busy putting food on trays.

"Today we'll have brunch on the patio," she announced.

The children helped her carry out fresh fruit, hot rolls, milk and pineapple fritters.

"Oh, it's all delicious," Nan remarked as they ate at tables by the pool.

"I'm having lime marmalade on my rolls *and* my fritters," said Flossie happily.

After brunch the children went to the side porch and worked on their stories and pictures. Flossie was coloring a flamingo.

"There, I'm finished!" she announced and flourished the picture in the air.

"Oh, that's good, Flossie," Susie cried. "See mine!" She held up a red macaw.

"It's bee-yoo-ti-ful," Flossie told her.

"Mine's going to be blue and yellow," Teddy announced.

"You know," Flossie remarked with pride, "I

really think the bird pictures are going to be wonderful. I never saw such pretty colors."

"Except on mice," said Freddie and they all giggled.

"I think I'll draw Mr. Click," Flossie decided.

"That's a good idea," Teddy said. "He ought to be in the book."

Meanwhile Dr. Funnybone had come out and walked over to the writers. Nan was pecking on the typewriter while Nellie and the two boys were writing furiously.

"This is fun," Charlie said. "Our mystery is so scary we're even scaring ourselves."

The doctor laughed. "That sounds good. Just keep working. Remember, you don't have much more time."

The next moment there was a loud *ACHOO!*

"Oh, there goes Flossie again," said Nan. The writers looked down the porch. The little girl was standing in front of the owl with her sketching pad and pencil. But before she could draw a line, she sneezed again.

Dr. Funnybone went over to her. "Come with me, Flossie," he said. "I want to look at your throat."

As Flossie followed him into his study, Susie jumped up and went with them.

"Is Flossie sick?" she asked anxiously.

The doctor looked into the little girl's throat. "No trouble there," he said.

Then he listened to her chest and took her temperature. "I can't find anything wrong," he said. "I think you have an allergy, Flossie. And since you don't have one at home, it must be something in Florida which is causing it. Now, what are you doing here that you don't do at home?"

"She eats lime marmalade," Susie spoke up.

The doctor nodded. "That could be it. Flossie, you leave the marmalade alone for a while. If you stop sneezing we'll know that was it."

"All right," said Flossie with a sigh. She and Susie went back to the porch and told the others about her allergy.

A little later the children put their work away carefully in the supply cabinet.

"My story is finished," said Nan happily. "The lady and the captain outwitted the pirates and escaped!"

The doctor smiled. "Then let's do something else. Boys, suppose we catch some fish." For the rest of the afternoon they dangled their lines off the dock.

The girls went to help the housekeeper. "Mama Luisa," said Flossie, "do you want to see the birds we drew?"

"Sure, sure."

Flossie ran off to get the pictures. Moments later she dashed back into the kitchen. "They're gone!" she cried.

"Your pictures?" asked Nan, surprised.

"Everything! The stories too!"

The girls ran to the supply cabinet. Everything was in order, but the book material was gone. They raced to the dock and told the fishermen.

The doctor looked grim. "Who would do such a thing?"

"Danny Rugg," said Teddy promptly. "After all, he kidnapped Mr. Click."

"We are not positive," Nan reminded him. "Besides, we can't accuse him of this without proof."

"Anyway, the spooks could have taken them," added Freddie. But no one could imagine why the mysterious prowlers would steal the stories and pictures.

For the next hour everyone searched high and low for the missing property. The older children went first to the gazebo, because that was where the owl had been found.

The boys removed more of the underseat lattice but saw nothing except a few old oil cans, a pair of rusty shears and a small wooden trunk with a broken handle.

Nan lifted the lid gingerly. The trunk was empty.

"There's nothing here," said Nellie when they had looked all around.

"The only thing we can do," Bert remarked at dinner, "is to start another batch of work and hope that the first one turns up."

"If it doesn't," said the doctor, "we're going to be in a spot. The publisher is waiting for my book with your stories in it."

"We'd better work tonight," said Nellie.

Everyone agreed. The doctor set up extra lamps on the porch and left the children to their task.

They worked for a while. Then Freddie said, "I think I'll draw a dolphin, but I need a picture to copy from. Did anybody bring a postcard from the Seaquarium?"

"I did," said his twin. "May I borrow your starfish, Teddy? I want to copy it."

"Sure," he said, busily drawing. "It's in the dresser."

"I know," said Freddie. "I'll get it."

The young twins went upstairs. The hall was dimly lit. As the children started down the hall, they stopped short. Two mice were running along, one pink, one blue!

"Mice!" the twins shouted.

"Follow them!" exclaimed Freddie.

He and Flossie dashed down the front stairs after the little animals. They ran across the hall into the dining room. The mice disappeared through the partly open door of a closet.

Freddie pulled it all the way open. The mice were gone. But on the floor in front of a mousehole were a blue sailboat and a pink toy dog.

Meanwhile, the other children had scattered through the house looking for Dr. Funnybone.

In a few minutes all the searchers gathered in the dining room. They had found no trace of the doctor.

"But look what we have!" exclaimed Flossie, holding up the dog. The young twins explained where they had discovered the toys.

"Maybe there's a clue on them," suggested Nan.

Freddie and Flossie examined the surprises. "There's a tag on the boat with the letters T-I-C on it," said Freddie.

"And here's one on the dog," said Flossie. "It says A-T."

"TIC and AT," said Nellie, puzzled. "What do they mean? It doesn't make sense."

"AT-TIC," the older twins cried out together. "That's it! We're supposed to go to the attic!"

"I know how," said Freddie. "There's a ladder on the wall by the back stairs. You go up through a little door in the ceiling."

The excited children dashed up to the second floor. The older boys got flashlights. Then Bert led the way up the ladder into the long, low room under the roof. It was hot and smelled musty.

"It's empty," said Charlie, disappointed.

"Not quite," Bert replied as his flashlight picked up an old radio on a small table. The children examined the odd, round-topped object with a worn cloth speaker in the front.

"That's really ancient," said Charlie. He

looked it over, inside and out. "Even the tubes are gone. It's dead as a doornail."

"But it must be a clue," said Nan. "It's the only thing up here."

While the others looked around the attic again, Bert glanced out a small window into the dark yard below. His heart jumped with excitement.

Was that a caped figure slipping out of the gazebo? The next moment it had vanished among the trees.

CHAPTER IX

By Zingo!

WHEN THE OTHER children left the attic, Bert drew Nan aside and told her about the figure.

"I'm not certain I saw it," he said, "but let's check the gazebo. We may find a clue."

The twins hurried down the back stairs and out into the yard. For a moment they stood watching and listening. All was still.

They walked quickly to the gazebo. Bert shone his light around. It was empty.

"The prowlers are searching for something here," said Bert, "but what can it be?"

He and Nan sat down and puzzled about it quietly. Suddenly they heard a rustle in the brush outside the gazebo.

"Put out your light!" came a sharp whisper from a man. "Do you want those kids to see you?"

Giving Nan's hand a warning squeeze, Bert obeyed.

"Sorry I'm late," the stranger went on. "I saw the skipper again in Miami. He'll meet us tomorrow at three o'clock in the Everglades on the walk into the wilderness area—the usual place. He wants double the money and the birds —or else!" Then the man said, "Did you get it?"

The twins' hearts were thumping hard. What should they do? Should they try to answer? The next moment they heard Teddy calling them.

"Let's go!" said the whisperer. "Come on!" The brush crackled as he hastened away.

The twins took a deep breath. "Wow!" said Bert. "That was close!"

"The man was expecting to meet somebody here," Nan remarked. "Probably the caped figure—you really did see it."

"Well, they're both gone now," said Bert. "We'd better leave. The others are looking for us."

As the twins stood up, Bert caught Nan's hand. "Wait," he said softly. "I thought I heard something outside the gazebo doorway."

For a moment the two listened intently but detected nothing. Had the prowler realized the mistake he had made? Had he come back to catch whoever was in the gazebo? The twins waited a little longer. There was no sound.

"I guess he's gone," said Nan. "It's safe to go out now."

She and Bert stepped out the door into the yard. The next moment a blanket fell over their heads and they were thrown to the ground. With muffled screams the twins struggled, but it was no use. Suddenly the heavy cover was yanked off. They were blinded by flashlights.

"Nan! Bert!" exclaimed Flossie.

The twins looked up into the dumfounded faces of Dr. Funnybone and the other children.

"We thought you were the spooks," the doctor explained.

"And we thought you were," said Bert as eager hands helped him and Nan to get up.

Back in the kitchen Nellie explained that she had looked out the window and seen a flashlight in the gazebo.

"We were sure you and Nan were still upstairs," said Freddie. "We called you."

"We were afraid to wait for fear the prowlers would get away," the doctor went on. "I grabbed the blanket from the couch in my study and we ran out there."

"Such excitement!" said Mama Luisa. "I think you need some food to make you feel better."

While Nellie and Flossie helped her serve milk and fudge cake, Nan told what she and Bert had overheard in the gazebo.

"If we could go to the Everglades tomorrow," said Bert, "we might spot Skipper Zingo and the spooks together."

"But how would we know them?" Nellie objected.

"We wouldn't," said Bert, "but Skipper Zingo cannot be a very friendly-looking man. If we see some mean-looking fellow wearing a captain's hat we might take a chance and spy on him."

"It's worth trying," the doctor agreed. "I'd like to get to the bottom of this Spanish ghost mystery."

Mama Luisa cleared her throat. "I do not want to interfere," she said politely, "but why don't you call the police?"

"Oh, no!" chorused the children.

"We want to solve it ourselves!" said Freddie.

"I would call the police," the doctor replied, "except that so far the spooks have not really done any harm. They are trespassing, that's all. If I ask the authorities to step in, the prowlers may run away. Then we might never find out what they're up to." He smiled. "More than anything, we all want to solve the mystery."

"How about the missing papers?" asked Mama Luisa.

"I'm afraid it is much more likely that Danny took them, though how we'll ever prove it I don't know," the doctor replied.

"Maybe you could talk to his aunt," Charlie suggested.

The doctor shook his head. "If Danny didn't do it, I would only be making more trouble for him. I'm afraid Danny is in enough already."

"Maybe we could get him to confess," said Freddie.

Flossie's eyes twinkled as she took the doctor's hand. "When are *you* going to confess, Dr. Funnybone?" The other children laughed.

"We think you know all about the colored mice and the toys in the closet," Freddie declared.

"Maybe I do, maybe I don't," said the doctor, smiling. "You're the detectives. You must find out." He stood up. "Now good night, everybody!"

The next morning, the children worked on the book. Right after lunch they piled into the minibus with Joe and started for Everglades National Park.

On the way they passed a sign which said: PLAY MINIATURE GOLF.

"Oh, can we do that, Joe, please?" begged Susie.

Joe glanced at his watch. "I guess you have time for one round."

A few minutes later he pulled into a parking lot beside a miniature golf course. "I'll wait here," he said as his passengers climbed out.

Chattering happily, the children paid and started through the small course.

"Everything is so cute," said Flossie. "I just love the tiny windmill and little ponds and castles!"

"You won't like it so much if you hit your ball into one of those ponds by mistake!" Nan teased her sister.

"I won't do that!" Flossie vowed.

All the children played well, but Freddie surprised the group when he made a hole-in-one!

"Good boy!" Bert praised him. "Most people take three strokes!"

"I'm going to be a golf pro someday," Freddie boasted.

Despite Freddie's skill Charlie won with the lowest score.

When they turned in their clubs and balls at the counter, Bert spotted some golf hats for sale. He purchased a red one and placed it on Freddie's head.

"That's to help you become a champion," Bert said.

"This is great," replied Freddie. "Thanks!"

An hour later they reached the Everglades National Park. Soon they saw an arrow pointing and a sign: *Wilderness Area*.

"This must be the place!" Nan exclaimed.

Joe turned into the road and in a few minutes came to a parking lot. The group left the car and started along a raised boardwalk. It curved between trees covered with vines. A glimmer of water could be seen between the slits in the boards.

"This is a swampy wilderness," Joe told them,

"where you will see plants and animals. But you must stay on the walks and keep together."

Bert checked his wrist watch. "It's quarter of three," he said. "Keep your eyes open for anybody who might be Skipper Zingo."

With Joe in the lead and Freddie last, the visitors walked through the swamp. Once Joe pointed to a white bird with a huge beak seated at the very top of a tree.

"That's a pelican," he said. "They make nests in treetops."

As they went on, Freddie took off his golf hat. He stuffed it in the pocket of his shorts, but it did not fit very well. He was too interested in the swamp to notice.

Looking from the wooden walk they could see dark water full of wide green lily leaves. Suddenly these parted and a large gray-green snout appeared, then the rest of the head, with two protruding eyes. The mouth opened wide showing sharp teeth.

"Yow! It's an alligator!" exclaimed Teddy.

At the same time something that looked like the top of a brown log rose from the water and another monster crawled onto the muddy bank.

"The place is full of them," said Joe. "You're safe as long as you stay on the raised walks."

The visitors went on. So far they had not seen anyone besides themselves. After a while Freddie felt for his hat. The souvenir was gone!

"Yow! It's an alligator!"
exclaimed Teddy.

"I must have dropped it," he thought, and hurried back along the walkway looking for the hat. "I hope it didn't fall in," he said to himself and glanced down at the murky water. Here and there he could see a brown snout peering out. As he rounded a bend, he ran straight into another sightseer.

"*Oof!*" the man grunted.

"Oh, excuse me!" said Freddie, stepping back.

As he looked up, he gave a frightened gasp. The man was Skipper York.

"You again!" he said angrily. "I'll teach you not to follow me! I'll dump you in with the alligators, by zingo!"

CHAPTER X

Dolphin Fun

FRIGHTENED, FREDDIE TURNED and ran back along the wooden walkway.

In a few moments he met Joe and the other children coming back to see what was the matter. Freddie blurted out his story.

"It's all right," said Joe. "York can't hurt you now."

"He said 'by Zingo!'" Freddie exclaimed. "I'll bet he says it all the time, so maybe it's his nickname."

"I'm sure you're right," Nan agreed. "Skipper York is Skipper Zingo."

"We'll go back," said Joe grimly. "I'd like to talk to him."

He took the lead and they walked back to the place where Freddie had seen the man. He was gone.

"We may as well go home," said Bert. "I don't

think any meeting will take place now. We probably scared them off."

The others agreed. They continued back along the wilderness trail in the way they had started. At the entrance Joe reported the man's threat to one of the rangers.

"We'll be on the lookout for him," the officer promised.

As the children and Joe crossed the parking lot, they saw a familiar car drive in.

"It's the photographers!" Bert exclaimed. The children hurried over as Jean and the two young men got out of the battered gray sedan.

"Hi!" Bert called.

"Did you come to take pictures?" asked Freddie eagerly.

The newcomers smiled and greeted everyone.

"We just found Skipper Zingo," said Nan excitedly. "He was in the swamp."

"We're pretty sure Skipper York is Zingo!" Bert explained.

"He came here to meet the spooks," Charlie added.

"And we've seen the ghost ship and been on the island," put in Flossie. "We have such a lot to tell you."

"We'd like to hear it," said Jean, patting the little girl's shoulder.

"But we really haven't time now," said Jon, glancing at his watch. He gave his sister a worried look. "We're late for an appointment."

"Okay," said Jean cheerfully. "Why don't you children come see us tomorrow afternoon? We don't live far from Dr. Funnybone. Palmetto Lane."

"I know where it is," Joe said.

"We're in the last trailer on the right," Jean told them. "Please come. We'd like to hear about all you've been doing and what you've found out."

"We sure would," Gus agreed.

Waving, the three hurried away as the others called good-by.

In the car on the way back Freddie looked glum. "I wish I hadn't lost my golf hat," he said.

"I'll bet I know who's wearing it," remarked Charlie with a grin.

"Who?" Freddie asked.

"Some alligator."

Even Freddie laughed at this as the other children giggled.

It was suppertime when the travelers reached home. They showered quickly. Then Teddy took his turn to ring the bell. While they hungrily ate fried chicken and biscuits with gravy they told the doctor all that had happened.

"Now you're getting somewhere!" he exclaimed. "I'll see what we can find out about this Skipper York. I have friends in Miami who might be able to help. I'll call them tonight."

After supper the older children went back to

work on their stories. The younger ones helped Dr. Funnybone feed Mr. Click his hamburger.

While Flossie was waiting eagerly for her turn she began sneezing. Alarmed, the owl spread his wings and flapped to the other end of the porch. Fluttering, he collapsed onto the typewriter.

"Mr. Click!" exclaimed Nan in surprise. "I can't type if you sit on the keys!"

Bert gently lifted the bird off the machine and carried him back to the doctor.

"He hasn't had much practice flying," said the physician, placing the owl on his shoulder. "He gets tired and soon falls down." He turned to Flossie, who was still sneezing. "You haven't had any lime marmalade today, have you, young lady?"

Flossie shook her head and sneezed again. Mr. Click blinked his eyes and clicked.

"And still she's sneezing," said Freddie, "so it can't be the marmalade that's causing it."

"Right," the doctor agreed.

"Oh, I'm glad," said the little girl, " 'cause now I can eat it again."

"What else have you eaten a lot of lately?" asked Dr. Funnybone.

"Fried bananas. Do I have to stop those?"

"Yes. If you sneeze anyway, we'll know it's something else."

"You're a detective, too, aren't you?" said Freddie.

"I'm a medical detective," the doctor said, smiling. "But I will be glad of any help you can give me."

Next morning the children worked hard on their new stories and pictures. Teddy was drawing a manta ray and Susie was making a diver in the Seaquarium tank. Freddie's dolphins were almost ready.

When Flossie finished coloring her starfish, she had an idea. Humming to herself, she drew busily for a while, then said, "Look what I made."

She held up her picture. The others laughed.

"It's an alligator wearing Freddie's golf hat!"

"That's cool," said Teddy. "I hope the doctor puts it in his book!"

At lunch they showed their work to Mama Luisa.

"You are very good artists," she said. Then she asked if they would like to see more live dolphins.

"Oh yes," said Susie. "Where are they?"

Mama Luisa replied that her cousin Pablo Garcia had a marina several miles up the road. "He has a pen with two tame dolphins in it."

"We're going to Palmetto Lane this afternoon," Nan told her.

"Why don't you stop there?" the housekeeper suggested. "It is right on the way. Wear bathing suits under your clothes," she told the older children. "You can swim with the dolphins."

After lunch the group walked up the road to Tavernier. As Dr. Funnybone had suggested, they rented bicycles and got on them. A short time later they saw the sign on a blue-roofed building down a side road: PABLO'S MARINA.

They pedaled along the dirt road and dismounted by the building. Nearby was a low board fence with a sign on it: *Dick and Dolly*. The children looked over the fence into a pool in which two dolphins were swimming.

A young dark-haired woman in a blue bathing suit came from the marina building. "I'm Mrs. Pablo Garcia," she said with a smile. "Do you older children want to swim with Dick and Dolly?"

"Yes!" Bert and Charlie chorused.

"Not me," Nellie said firmly. "They're too big."

"Umm, I don't know," Nan looked doubtful. Then she decided. "All right."

The boys quickly peeled off their jeans and shirts and jumped into the water. Nan followed more slowly. She stood and watched as the boys moved toward the big mammals. Soon her brother and Charlie were laughing and dodging as the creatures swam past them.

Suddenly one of the dolphins came near Nan. She patted his gray side timidly. "It feels like rubber," she said and giggled nervously.

The next moment the other dolphin dived under her. With a cry she rose from the water on

With a cry Nan rose from the water!

the animal's back and then fell off as he went
under again. The other dolphin swam swiftly
past and bounced Charlie sideways.

"I want to get out!" Nan cried. She hurried
to the side and scrambled from the pool. The
boys followed in a few minutes, breathless and
laughing.

"That was fun!" said Bert.

"I was scared," Nan admitted.

Mrs. Garcia smiled. "Dick and Dolly play
rough sometimes," she said. "But they're really
very friendly. There are many legends about
dolphins saving drowning people. I'm going to
feed them now," she added. "Would you like to
help?"

The younger children said they would, and
Nellie and Charlie nodded.

"I'd like to," said Bert, "but we promised to
go see someone this afternoon."

Nan noticed that the others looked disappointed. "Why don't the rest of you stay here?"
she said. "Bert and I will go to Palmetto Lane.
We'll meet you back home."

"That's a good idea," said Freddie.

Mrs. Garcia walked to a wooden tub full of
fresh fish. "If you hold one of these over the
edge of the pool, Dolly or Dick will take it
from you," she said to the little boy.

Then she led Bert and Nan inside the marina
and showed them places to change from their
wet suits into dry clothes.

When they came out, Flossie was just holding a fish over the fence. The next moment a dolphin leaped up and took it from her hand.

"Oh, that's fun!" the little girl squealed.

Bert and Nan rode away on their bicycles. They could hear the others laughing and calling excitedly from the marina.

The twins pedaled ten minutes along the main road before they came to a wooden sign saying: PALMETTO LANE. It was bordered by rows of house-trailers with bright-colored awnings and chairs outside.

"There's Jon!" Nan exclaimed.

The photographer was standing on the bluff at the end of the road. As Bert drew closer he saw that there was a canal at the foot of it.

"Hi!" called Bert and put on a burst of speed.

When he was almost at the bluff, he tried to use his brakes. They did not work!

The bicycle shot toward the canal! "Help!" Bert yelled.

CHAPTER XI

Help Yourself!

"HOLD IT!" cried Jon. Jumping forward, he managed to grab the bicycle by the rear fender.

"Thanks!" Bert exclaimed as he dismounted. "Something's happened to these brakes."

Jon examined the bicycle. "I'm not surprised. This thing's pretty old," he remarked. "We'll give you a lift back to the bike shop when you go."

Bert wheeled the machine to a blue trailer, where Jean and Nan were talking in the yard.

"We almost had to pull you out of the canal, Bert," Jean teased him. Bert grinned.

"You live close to the water," Nan remarked. "Do you have a boat?"

"Yes," said Jon, "but Gus is using it right now." He pointed to a yellow trailer across the lane. "He lives over there."

"Come and have some cookies and soda." Jean

led the way to a small patio under an awning. While she went into the trailer Jon explained that he, his sister and Gus had been friends from childhood. "Jean graduated from high school last June, Gus and I the summer before. We're taking a year off before college to do some free-lance photography."

Jean heard him as she came out with a tray of refreshments. "We like Florida," she said, "because it's warm and sunny and has so many beautiful scenes to photograph." She passed the cookies and cold drinks. "Now please tell us about your mystery."

"First of all," said Nan, "as we told you yesterday, we're pretty sure that Skipper York is Skipper Zingo." She explained what had happened in the Everglades.

Jon and Jean exchanged glances. "Yes, you're right," said Jon. "Zingo is his nickname. We've heard him called that."

Bert and Nan told the Tomsons what had happened.

"You've learned a lot," Jean remarked. She and Jon looked very much impressed.

"But we don't know what the spooks are after," Bert admitted.

"Wouldn't it be better to give up trying to find out?" said Jon. "You know, it could be dangerous."

"Oh, we don't want to quit," Bert declared firmly. "We love to solve mysteries."

"Yes, we can see that," said Jean with a smile.

Suddenly Bert asked, "The boat that Gus has now—is it the one you rented from Skipper York?"

"No," said Jon. "We're using York's boat to do some special photography."

Bert was about to ask where the boat was, but Jean spoke up. "Would you like more soda?"

Nan shook her head. "No, thank you, we'd better be going."

"We'll drive you back to the bicycle shop," Jon offered.

While he and Bert lifted the two bikes into the trunk of the gray sedan, Nan helped Jean carry in the glasses and the cookie plate. She looked admiringly around the clean, tidy trailer.

"Oh," she said surprised, "what are those?"

Several swords and a Spanish helmet were propped in one corner.

Jean smiled. "Those are Jon's. He collects old armor."

Before Nan could see any more of the trailer, Jean led the way outside. They got into the sedan and drove to the bicycle shop in Tavernier. Jon and Bert unloaded the bicycles. A tall, skinny boy of about sixteen came out of the shop.

"Hi, Buzz," said Jon.

"Hi," the other answered.

Bert asked to see the owner.

"Not here," said the boy. Bert explained that the bicycle's brakes had frozen.

"Guess I'll have to charge you for the damage," Buzz told him.

"Oh no, you won't," Jon said firmly. "That bike is too old—it isn't safe. You're lucky my friend wasn't hurt. It wasn't his fault the brakes failed."

Buzz shrugged. "He broke them."

"I know the owner of this place," said Jon. "He'd never approve of this. I think I'll find him and tell him about it."

The boy bit his lip and looked at the strapping, stern-faced young man before him. "All right," he said. "Forget it."

Sulkily he wheeled the bicycles away. Bert thanked Jon for his help.

"That's okay," the young photographer said. "Get back in the car and I'll take you home."

He drove the twins to Dr. Funnybone's place and let them off at the driveway. The twins thanked the Tomsons and Nan added, "Wouldn't you like to come in?"

"Some other time," Jean said with a smile.

"They're nice," said Nan as she and Bert walked up the drive. "I wonder what kind of photography they're doing. They seemed sort of mysterious about it."

"Probably something special," said Bert. "Speaking of mysteries," he went on, "I've been thinking about the colored animals. That radio in the attic must be a clue and I think I know what it means." He told Nan his idea.

His twin giggled. "The next time Dr. Funny-bone tries his trick, we'll know just what to do!"

That evening, the doctor drove the children to the movies in the minibus.

Afterward he said, "How would you like to visit the ship on which Columbus sailed to America?"

"Where is it?" Teddy asked.

"About a mile from here," the doctor answered.

His passengers piled into the minibus and soon saw a strange sight. In the middle of a big parking lot stood a large sailing ship ablaze with lights. A neon sign on it said:

SANTA MARIA ICE CREAM SHOP.

The children got out and followed the doctor over to the colorful craft.

"This isn't really Columbus' ship, of course," the doctor explained as they walked up the gangplank. "It's just a copy."

"It doesn't seem large enough to have come all the way across the ocean," Charlie remarked.

"No," the doctor agreed. "It was not nearly so big as a galleon."

"This size boat was called a caravel," said Bert, who had learned this fact in school.

The high sides of the boat were sturdily built. Near the bow were carved life-sized wooden heads. One was of a bearded man.

"The caravel had nice decorations," said Nan.

"Yes," the doctor replied. "And galleons were

even fancier. They had fine furnishings and beautiful carvings and figures."

As they stepped onto the deck, the children saw dozens of tables and chairs. A smiling waitress hurried over and with Bert's help put two tables together for the large party.

"Do you want to give me your order," she asked, "or make your own sundaes?"

"Make our own," chorused the children.

The waitress pointed to a sheltered area at one end of the deck. "You will find our Help-Yourself-Bar there." She smiled. "It's in the same place where Columbus' sailors would have cooked their meals."

The children hurried over and joined the line of people making their own sundaes. The young twins were last.

Each child took a dish. A white-coated attendant put a large scoop of ice cream in it.

"Now you move down the line," the waiter said, smiling, "and help yourself to any flavor syrup, whipped cream, nuts, cherries, colored sprinkles—anything you want."

"I think I'll take chocolate," said Freddie.

"Oh, it all looks so yummy!" Flossie exclaimed. "I think I'll take marshmallow syrup."

She ladled a gooey white covering over the ice cream. "And now whipped cream," she thought happily. But as she reached for the squirt can, someone snatched it.

Surprised, she turned. Danny Rugg was right behind her!

Sssskkkt! He squirted a blob of cream right onto her nose. "Ha-ha!" Danny snickered.

"Stop!" cried Flossie.

Freddie turned. "Danny Rugg!"

Sssskkkt! A blob of whipped cream hit Danny in the eye as Freddie angrily aimed his squirt can.

"Okay, Freddie!" said Danny. "Here it comes!" He sprayed a whipped cream mustache on each of the small twins.

As Flossie screamed, Freddie angrily shot a stream of cream into Danny's hair. The older boy yelled, grabbed a handful of cherries and backed off. As he began throwing them, a middle-aged man with glasses seized his arm. He wore a large button which said *Manager*.

"I'll have no roughhousing here, young man," he said.

Danny turned away, mumbling under his breath.

At that moment Dr. Funnybone ran up. "What's going on here?" The children had never heard his voice so stern. "Freddie, Flossie, you know better."

Tears filled Flossie's eyes. "Danny started it," she said. Excitedly Freddie told the doctor what the big boy had done.

"I did not," said Danny loudly over and over.

The whipped cream battle was on!

"Yes, he did," said his aunt as she pushed in from the sidelines. Her face was red with embarrassment. "I saw the whole thing. I'm so sorry," she said to the manager and Dr. Funnybone. "I don't know what I'm going to do with Danny."

"I must ask you not to bring him here again, madam," said the manager coldly.

"What do I care?" said Danny. "I'm going home soon anyway."

"Come along, Danny," said Mrs. Rugg grimly. She paid her bill and led him away.

Sheepishly the small twins helped the manager clean up the mess. Then they finished making their sundaes and ate them.

"We're sorry about the fight, Dr. Funnybone," Freddie apologized.

The doctor sighed. "It wasn't the right thing to do, you know that. But I must admit that Danny is enough to make anybody fighting mad."

"I'd just like to know what he did with our pictures and stories," said Nan. "I feel sure he took them!"

That night when the girls went to bed, Susie said, "Well, one nice thing. We know Danny doesn't have a chance to sleep in a water bed. All he has is a plain old mattress!"

"Let's forget about him," Nellie advised, turning off the light. "I'm sick of Danny Rugg!"

Just when they were drifting off to sleep, the kitchen bell began ringing.

"The alarm signal!" cried Nan. "That means everybody come quickly!"

CHAPTER XII

Rickety Tree House

THE GIRLS PULLED on their robes and hurried into the hall.

"What's the matter?" exclaimed Bert as the boys burst from their room. From below they could hear Mama Luisa's excited cries.

"Look!" yelled Charlie.

Down the hall came a yellow kitten, a red striped rabbit, two polka-dot puppies and some colored mice! The younger children screamed in excitement.

"This is our chance!" whispered Bert to Nan. "Come with me!"

He dashed down the back stairs and across the kitchen to the hallway. Sure enough! The light showed beneath the closet door under the staircase!

Bert put his finger to his lips. Very quietly he

took hold of the handle, then jerked the door open!

Dr. Funnybone was standing before a control board full of dials and knobs!

"We've guessed your secret!" exclaimed Nan.

Startled, the doctor whirled. Then he laughed. "So you have! How did you catch on?"

Before the twins could explain, Mama Luisa came running from the back of the house. She laughed as the excited children streamed into the kitchen, each carrying a brightly colored toy.

"I followed the rabbit into the bathroom!" Nellie cried, "and look what I found!" She held up a huge, red-striped candy cane.

Charlie ran in carrying a yellow beach ball. "I chased the kitten to the coat closet," he said.

Teddy had an orange dump truck and Susie a small doll wearing a purple dress. They had followed the mice to the front porch.

"We chased the polka-dot puppies to the dining room," said Flossie, "and found these." She and Freddie held up green bones.

"They're flashlights," Freddie explained. He beamed one around the room.

"We're giving them to you and Bert," said Flossie as she handed hers to Nan, " 'cause we already found toys."

Just then Nellie spotted the open closet door. "What are all those knobs and buttons, Dr. Funnybone?"

"Let Nan and Bert tell you," he said, smiling.

Bert explained that he had felt sure the radio in the attic was a clue.

"I finally decided it was meant to give us a hint that the little animals were radio controlled. Some place in the house Dr. Funnybone had to have a control panel from which he could operate each animal."

"Bert once noticed a light under this closet door," said Nan. "And we thought it was suspicious that the door was always locked."

"I set up this trick years ago," the doctor said, "when my own children were small."

He reached in his pocket and took out a blue mouse.

"Each creature has a radio unit inside," he said. "They're made of plastic and plush so they look lifelike."

" 'Cept for the colors," said Susie, giggling.

"They come through a little door in the baseboard at the top of the back stairs," said Charlie. "Am I right?"

The doctor laughed. "So you spotted that?"

"Nan did," Charlie admitted.

"It works by radio," the doctor explained. "The animals are kept in a cabinet in my control room. They go up a narrow pipe within the walls and out the little door."

He said that each little animal went to the place where he sent it, then disappeared into another hole. Afterward, when no one was around, the doctor returned to the control room. He made the creatures run back through the door in the upper hall and down into the cabinet.

"The house has hidden microphones in it, too," he went on, "so I always knew from your voices who would be seeing the animal. I decided it was time now to end the joke. I asked Mama Luisa to ring the bell so you would all come down and see the animals."

"We really thank you," said Nan. "It was such fun!" The others added their thanks.

"Oh!" exclaimed Charlie. "I just had the greatest idea! Why don't we invite Danny over and trick him with these animals—I can just see his face!"

"Will you teach us how to operate them?" Bert asked the doctor eagerly.

"Indeed I will," he replied. "Danny is certainly due for a surprise."

Dr. Funnybone gave Bert and Charlie a quick lesson on the control board. Thinking happily of their party for Danny, the children trooped off to bed.

Next morning Mama Luisa was wearing a dark blue dress with a necklace and earrings as she served breakfast.

"It is my day off," she told them, "and I am going to see my sister in Miami."

"I also have to go," said the doctor. "The publisher of my book is there on vacation and wants to see me. I'll drive Mama Luisa in my car. We'll be back tomorrow afternoon. Meanwhile, Joe is in charge. He will sleep here in his mother's room."

When Joe arrived, the doctor backed his little red sportscar out of the garage. Mama Luisa climbed in. "Now everybody be good." She smiled and waved as the car drove off.

While Nan told Joe the plan about Danny, Bert called Mrs. Rugg's house. The boy's aunt answered and Bert explained that the children wanted Danny to come over for a "making up" party. Danny did not want to come, but Mrs. Rugg insisted.

"I asked him for tomorrow afternoon," Bert reported to the others with a grin. "That'll give us plenty of time to practice the controls."

"Ye-ah!" said Charlie and rubbed his hands together happily.

Nan spoke up. "How about exploring the island today? We've never had a look at it in daylight."

"The tide'll be out now," said Joe. "We'll go this afternoon. During the morning you can work on the book."

"Susie and I want to draw gulls," said Flossie. "But we need pictures to copy from."

Joe suggested that he take them over to the

mud flats some miles away. "There you can see real gulls."

"May Nan and I go too?" Nellie asked.

"Sure thing," said Joe. "How about you other children?"

Freddie and Teddy wanted to, but the older boys decided to work at home on their new stories.

Five minutes later the minibus was humming up the main road. Soon Joe turned off and they wound along wooded back roads until the trees thinned out. They stopped on the edge of a huge, flat area with blue water beyond.

"The ground's in pieces!" exclaimed Freddie. "Like a puzzle!"

"That's mud," said Joe. "The soil gets wet and when it dries, cracks into those large plates."

"Is it dry enough to walk on?" asked Nan.

"Most of it," Joe replied. "Some pieces may still be a little damp from the tide."

Carrying notebooks and pencils, the children walked out on the odd gray ground and looked around curiously.

"There's a bird," said Flossie, "on that tall stick in the water."

"That's a heron," said Joe. "The stick is a channel marker. We need them because the water is shallow."

"There are lots of gulls," said Susie. She moved closer to a large plump gray-and-white bird standing near the water's edge.

While the young children were busy drawing, Nan and Nellie looked around. Suddenly Nellie spotted a number of deep footprints in the softer mud.

"Look!" she said. "What big feet!"

Joe came over and stared at the prints. "They look like heavy boot marks."

Nan examined them. She picked out fragments of black material crushed in one of the marks. "Lace!" she exclaimed.

"Lace!" Joe repeated. "Who would bring anything that fancy out here?"

Nan thought at once of the singing ghost. "She wore a black mantilla and often they're made of lace. I think the spooks were here!"

"You're right, I'll bet," said Joe.

Nan borrowed his pocket knife and carefully dug up one of the large mud plates with a print on it. Nellie wrapped the lace in paper and put it in her pocket.

As Joe and the others were leaving the mud flats, the girls told the younger children of their discovery. Flossie glanced back and saw a black motorboat roaring across the bay.

"Why would anybody want an all-black boat?" she remarked. "It's not very pretty."

"That's true," Joe said. "But often people who are doing something underhanded paint their boats black and run without lights. That way they can carry on their business at night."

"Maybe that's how the spooks get to Silver

"The spooks were here!" said Nan.

Key," said Nan. "I've been wondering why we never see boat lights around there at night."

The children gazed at the black boat, but it was too far away to see the people in it.

Later at the house, Nan and Nellie showed Bert and Charlie the clues they had found.

"Let's take the footprint to the island with us," Bert suggested. "If we find one like it there, we can be sure this was made by the spooks."

After lunch all the children worked hard on their stories and pictures. At three o'clock they set out for the island.

When they arrived, Joe dropped anchor at the water's edge and they stepped ashore.

"We have two hours until the tide turns," he said. "We must be back here by then, or we might be stranded."

Quietly the party moved into the dark green jungle. With Bert leading and Joe last, they followed a rough path under low-hanging branches and vines.

Suddenly Joe gave a low whistle. "Come here," he called softly.

The others turned back, but Nan had caught sight of a platform up in a tree. A wooden ladder was nailed to the trunk. Peering upward, Nan thought she saw a bit of black lace caught on a broken board. Or was it leaf shadows? Cautiously she climbed the ladder and crawled onto the rickety platform.

CRACK! The boards gave way!

"Help!" Nan cried as she fell through the floor!

CHAPTER XIII

Friendly Spooks

As NAN CRASHED through the rotten platform, she caught the edge of a board. Hanging from it, she was afraid to drop into the thick underbrush. There might be snakes!

"Help!" she called.

The next moment Nan heard something crashing through the brush below but could see no one. At the same time she spotted Bert, Charlie and Joe running pell-mell toward the tree. The others followed.

"We're coming!" called her twin. Instantly the crashing footsteps died away.

"Where are you?" Charlie yelled.

"Up here!"

"Let go," Joe ordered. "We'll catch you!"

Nan dropped. Strong arms caught her and set her on the ground.

"Thanks," Nan said. "Listen! There's someone else on the island!" She told about the noise she had heard.

"It was probably one of the spooks," said Bert.

"Oh, he almost caught you, Nan." Flossie shivered.

The other children looked around uneasily.

"What were you doing in the tree?" Nellie whispered.

Nan explained about the tree house and the piece of lace she thought she had seen.

"I'll check," Charlie offered.

Quickly but carefully he climbed the ladder to the edge of the platform. He scanned the boards for a few minutes, then came down.

"It must have been a shadow," he reported.

"Who do you suppose built that little house?" Susie asked.

Joe grinned. "I did."

"You did!" the children chorused.

"No fooling?" asked Freddie.

"No fooling." Joe smiled. "Some other boys and I used to play over here years ago. We put that platform up there for a clubhouse."

"You must have had fun," said Freddie.

Bert asked, "Did you ever find any parts of the old wreck?"

"I didn't," Joe replied, "but one of the other boys said he once saw the arm of a statue among some mangrove roots. It still had traces of gold paint on it."

"Is the arm still there?" Bert asked.

"No. A big storm was coming up and my friend couldn't stay to pry the statue loose. When he went back with his brother to get it, the arm was gone. It probably had been washed out to sea again. Violent storms sometimes toss up things that have been underwater and other storms wash away what has been on land."

"It sounds as if parts of the wreck could still be nearby underwater," Bert declared.

"If we keep our eyes open," said Nellie, "maybe we'll find something too."

Freddie spoke up. "Guess what Joe found, Nan—a hermit crab."

He opened his hand and showed a snail shell. "Come out, Mr. Hermit," the little boy said and shook the shell. A tiny tan creature emerged, then scooted back inside.

"They often live in other animals' shells," said Joe. "This little fellow found an empty house and moved in."

Nan's mind was not on the crab. "I've been thinking about the footsteps I heard. Don't you think we should try to find out who else is on the island?"

"Maybe whoever you heard has gone to the big clearing," Bert suggested.

"All right," said Joe. "But we'll only take a look at him—nothing else!"

Charlie spoke up. "If the guy's alone we could capture him."

"No," said Joe firmly. "Not with the little children along. He might be dangerous. I'll lead the way," he added.

They started single-file along the path. Once, as they crossed a gully, Susie lost her shoes in the mud. It took awhile to fish them out, wipe them off and clean her feet. More time was lost when Joe made a long detour around a swampy spot.

At last they reached the clearing. It was empty. But most of the weeds had been trampled.

"The spooks have been here for sure," Joe remarked.

"Let's go on," Bert urged. "Maybe we'll find one of them."

Joe glanced doubtfully at his watch. "We haven't time," he said. "If we start back now, we'll get to the beach before the tide turns."

"We can come another day," Nan suggested.

On the way to the shore, Freddie put the hermit crab back under the mangrove root where Joe had found him.

When they stepped out of the jungle onto the beach, they could not believe their eyes. The motorboat was on the sand. Only the very tip of the stern was in water!

A brisk wind was blowing.

"Oh, no!" cried Joe and slapped his forehead. "The tide turned early!"

He called their attention to the brisk wind that was blowing. Then he explained that when the water is shallow, a strong wind often helps to blow the tide out.

"It goes faster then, of course," said Joe. "Quick!" he ordered, "everybody push the boat! Maybe we can float it yet!"

Everybody pushed hard, but the heavy craft would not move. With each lap of the waves, the water ebbed farther out.

"Dig under it!" cried Bert. "Maybe we can let water run underneath to float it off."

As the younger children scooped furiously with their hands, the others tried to push. But it was no use. At last they sat back on their heels exhausted. The boat was high and dry.

"What'll we do now?" Charlie asked.

"We'll just have to wait until the tide comes in again," Joe replied.

"It'll be dark by then," Bert said.

The younger children looked frightened. "I don't want to stay on this spooky island at night," Flossie wailed.

"Maybe we could light a fire and send up smoke signals," said Nan. "Somebody might come and get us."

The next moment there was a sudden loud crackling in the bushes.

"The spooks!" Susie screamed and threw her arms around Nan.

"Hush!" said Bert sharply. "Listen!"

A woman was singing softly in Spanish. Gradually the sound moved farther away.

"Maybe we can float it off!"
cried Bert.

"Let's try to get a look at her," Bert said. "Please, Joe."

The older boy looked worried. "The little ones are scared," he said.

"They can stay here," Nellie proposed.

"No!" chorused the young ones.

"If we all stick together," said Bert, "I feel sure we'll be safe. We'll keep the younger children surrounded."

"I won't be scared," Freddie declared bravely, "if we're all together."

"Okay," said Joe.

As quietly as possible he and the children went back into the jungle. Now and then Joe held up his hand and they stopped to listen. The song went on, but always farther away.

"It's really a very pretty song," Nan whispered.

"I have a feeling that she's leading us on a wild goose chase," said Bert. "We never get any closer to her."

"And we're going farther and farther from the shore," Charlie pointed out. "Maybe something is going on there that the spooks don't want us to see."

"I thought of that, too," said Joe. "We'd better go back. I'd hate to have anything happen to the doctor's motorboat."

The nine detectives turned around and made their way back to the beach. Another surprise awaited them!

"Look at the boat!" Nan exclaimed. "It's floating!"

They ran over to the water's edge. There was a shallow gully in the sand where the boat had been pulled off. Alongside it were two sets of boot prints.

"These look like the ones on the mud flats!" Nan exclaimed.

She slipped off her shoes, waded to the boat and took a paper bag from one of the seats. Carefully she slipped out the mud sample and placed it next to the prints on the sand. They matched perfectly.

"These fellows must have attached a rope to the bow and pulled the boat off with another motorboat," Joe decided.

As he and the children splashed out to the *Flying Lime,* Charlie remarked that the spooks had done them a favor.

"And maybe the one Nan heard was really going to help her down from the tree," said Flossie.

Joe nodded. "Perhaps they are friendly spooks after all."

But as he lifted Flossie into the boat, she exclaimed. "Look! Here's a note!"

On the red leather seat was a piece of bark. A skull was drawn on it in heavy pencil. Under it were the words: KEEP AWAY!

CHAPTER XIV

Danny's Big Day

"THAT'S NOT A friendly note," said Bert grimly as he climbed into the boat. "We'd better not count on the spooks being harmless."

"I guess they only floated our boat in order to get us off the island," Charlie remarked.

Moments later the *Flying Lime* was speeding toward the mainland. It was nearly sundown when they reached home. Joe unlocked the back door and they all went into the kitchen.

Teddy and Susie hurried off through the doctor's study to the side porch to see Mr. Click. To their surprise he was awake. The owl walked restlessly back and forth on his perch, opening and closing his beak.

"He's hungry, I guess," said Teddy. "Something must have waked him early." He went to the kitchen and took some raw hamburger from the refrigerator. Patiently he and Susie fed the bird.

After a quick swim the children put on clean clothes and came to help prepare supper. Before Joe changed, he had lit the patio grill. The boys took steaks from the refrigerator and carried out bowls of salad which Mama Luisa had left.

"Ooh, I just love potato chips," Susie announced, as she helped Freddie empty a big bag of them into a large bowl.

"I do too," Freddie added, taking another handful.

"If you two start on those," Nan warned, "there won't be any left."

Soon the meat was sizzling over the coals and before long the hungry group began to eat. Afterward Nan got ice cream bars from the freezer and passed them around.

When it was dark Bert and Charlie lit the patio lights. For a long time they all sat talking about the mystery.

"Skipper Zingo must be very sure those silver birds are on the island," said Nellie. "Otherwise why would he go to so much trouble looking for them there?"

Nan agreed. "He must know where the captain's wife hid the birds, and he must have pretty good reason to believe that the part of the ship where she hid them was washed ashore on the island."

"Maybe," said Joe. "Treasure hunters are

funny. Some of them just go ahead on wild hunches."

"I feel sorry for Gus and the Tomsons," Bert spoke up. "Skipper Zingo's going to make trouble for them, I'm afraid."

Nan saw Flossie yawn. "Time to go to bed, I guess," she said. "Don't forget, tomorrow Danny is coming."

Freddie glanced up at the house. In the window of the boys' bedroom he thought he saw a figure.

"Who went upstairs?" Freddie asked sleepily.

"Nobody," Charlie replied. "We're all here."

Freddie sat bolt upright and looked harder at the dark screen. The figure was gone. "I thought I saw somebody up in our window."

Flossie shivered. "Stop trying to scare us, Freddie," she said.

"I'm not," he replied. "I really thought I saw somebody."

"Can't be," said Charlie. "No one's going to prowl around inside a house with nine people at home!"

The youngsters carried the dishes inside and washed them. Meanwhile Joe made sure the fire in the grill was out.

As Bert turned off the last patio lamp, he looked across the bay. "The mist is rising," he remarked.

The next moment, out of the fog slid the ghostly hulk of the galleon.

Freddie gasped and the others watched speechless as it disappeared in another patch of mist.

"Wow!" whispered Charlie. "It sure is a weird sight."

"If there were somebody here to stay with the little ones, we could go after it," said Joe. "But not this time. Besides, the fog makes it dangerous to take our boat out."

Disappointed, they went into the house and told the girls what they had seen.

"Where do you think the spooks keep the galleon hidden?" Nan asked.

"There are several deep coves on the other side of the island," said Joe. "Maybe in one of those."

"We'll just have to go over that key thoroughly," said Bert.

Susie pulled Joe's sleeve. "Before we go to bed, could we please feed Mr. Click again?"

"Okay," he said. "Let's get a little raw meat from the refrigerator."

As the four younger children went with Joe to feed the owl, the older ones started upstairs. When the boys entered their room and turned on the light, they stopped short.

"Oh-oh!" said Charlie. "Somebody *has* been in here! All the bureau drawers are pulled out!"

The boys ran into the hall, called the girls and quickly explained.

"A prowler! Freddie was right!" said Nellie.

"Maybe he's still in the house!" Nan cried out.

While Bert and Charlie began checking the second floor rooms, the girls hurried down to the porch to inform the others.

"All of you stay right here!" Joe ordered sharply. "Don't leave each other, and sing out if you see anybody! I'll go—"

At that moment they heard the back screen door squeak. Joe raced around to the rear porch with the children at his heels.

"There he goes!" cried Freddie, pointing into the yard. A dark figure was dashing down the path toward the shore!

At the same time Bert and Charlie came running onto the porch from the kitchen.

"Catch him!" Joe cried.

He and the older boys raced out the back door, across the yard and down the path. The fog was drifting in from the bay. As they neared the water, they could see nothing. Once Bert bumped into Charlie and both almost fell.

"Hold it!" said Joe. "This is hopeless."

The boys agreed. Disappointed, the three made their way back to the house. The others were in the front hall.

"I've been thinking," Nan spoke up, "that the prowler must have been in here when we

"Catch him!" Joe cried.

got home from the island. Remember how up-set the owl was? Probably the fellow woke him up."

"He must have got in through the study door," Susie suggested, " 'cause it was open when we went to feed Mr. Click the first time."

"We thought somebody forgot to lock it," said Teddy.

Bert and Joe hurried to check the door. They reported that the lock had been broken.

"Once we were in the house the prowler was afraid to try to slip out," said Nellie. "But why didn't he sneak out the front when we were on the patio?"

"Because we were talking about the mystery," Charlie decided. "He was listening from our window."

"I wonder who the man was," said Teddy.

"One of the spooks or Skipper Zingo," said Bert.

"He must have been looking for something," Charlie said. "But what?"

"There's nothing in those drawers but clothes," Bert declared.

"You'd better get some sleep," Joe broke in. "Tomorrow is Danny's big day!"

After the younger children were in bed, Joe and the older ones checked once more to be sure that no one was in the house and that the front and back doors were locked. They wired the study door closed and moved the couch in front of it.

Next morning after breakfast Bert, Nan and Charlie went down the path looking for clues. Along the shore they found several narrow footprints in damp sand and followed them to the next property. There, beyond a clump of bushes, was a path of oil on the water.

"This is probably where he had a motorboat hidden," Bert said.

"I have a hunch it was Skipper Zingo," Nan added. "He's a small, thin man and that footprint is short and narrow."

The rest of the morning the older children wrote more of their stories while the younger ones colored pictures. At lunch, Freddie's thoughts seemed to be far away. Suddenly he said, "After Danny chases the animals, we ought to serve sundaes."

"Regular ice cream sundaes?" Flossie asked.

Freddie grinned. "Well, not exactly." As he told them his idea, the others laughed.

"But we'll need your help, Joe," said Bert. "Will you do it?"

"Will I do it?" asked Joe with a grin. "Come with me!" He led Freddie to Mama Luisa's room and gave him what was needed.

Promptly at two o'clock Mrs. Rugg drove up and let Danny out at the front door. Nan and the others greeted him.

"Where's Bert?" asked Danny.

"He's busy on a job right now," said Nan. "You see, we have a mystery here. The house seems to be overrun by pink and blue mice and green polka-dot dogs."

"That's a stupid joke," said Danny. "There's no such thing as blue mice."

The next moment a blue mouse shot down the front stairs. Before Danny could speak, colored animals came running down one after the other.

"Wha-what's going on?" Danny asked in disbelief.

"If you catch one," said Nan, "you get a prize."

Danny began to chase the creatures. Up and downstairs he ran, in and out of rooms, but always the little animals escaped. At last Danny collapsed on the bottom step of the staircase.

"It's no use. Nobody can catch those things."

"Forget it, Danny," said Charlie. "It's just a little game Dr. Funnybone thought up for us. Come on and have some refreshments."

As they walked down the hall, Bert stepped out of the closet.

"How did you pull that crazy trick?" asked Danny.

"It's Dr. Funnybone's secret, so I can't tell you."

In the kitchen the girls had set the big round table with bowls, spoons and napkins. As Nan dished out the ice cream, Flossie and Susie put out a cup of cherries and a pitcher of syrup. Nellie took a large blue bowl of fluffy white cream from the refrigerator.

As they all sat down, Nan said, "We thought we'd make our own sundaes, 'cause that's more fun."

Nellie passed everybody extra big paper napkins. "It might be messy," she said with a smile.

Everyone poured chocolate syrup on the ice cream. Then Freddie picked up the blue bowl and passed it to Danny.

"Company first," he said.

All the children watched as Danny took an enormous helping. On top of the white pyramid he put three cherries. Then he took a huge spoonful and put it in his mouth.

A strange expression crossed his face and he jumped up with a cry!

CHAPTER XV

Walk the Plank!

QUICKLY NAN AND NELLIE shoved extra napkins to Danny.

"Oooo—UGH—eee!" He made strange noises as he dashed to the sink and rinsed his mouth with water. The other children were giggling.

"Shaving cream!" exploded Danny when he could speak. "That was a mean trick!"

"We thought it was a good one," Charlie said. "It's a lot funnier than those you played on us!"

Joe had appeared in the kitchen doorway to watch. "It's better than making a bus go off the road, Danny," he said.

"Or putting cream mustaches on Flossie and me," Freddie added.

"We didn't really hurt you, Danny," Flossie explained, "but you could have hurt the owl.

Suppose we'd never found the poor little thing."

"I don't know what you're talking about," Danny protested. "I didn't take any owl."

"We can prove it," Bert told him. "We found one of your gumdrops. You must have left sticky fingerprints all over the lattice." The big boy turned red. "Besides," Bert went on, "sneaking in people's houses is against the law."

Danny looked worried. "I didn't mean anything bad. I came over to see you and nobody was around. The porch door was open and I didn't think it would matter if I just looked around a little. The owl was asleep. It was just a joke," he insisted. "All I did was hide the owl and borrow a bunch of old stories and pictures!"

There was a gasp from the others.

"So!" exclaimed Bert. "You *did* take our book material!"

Immediately Danny saw his mistake. But he tried to bluff it out. "So what?"

"You tell us where they are, Danny Rugg!" demanded Nellie.

"I will not!"

"You will, too," chorused the younger children.

"You can't make me!" said Danny. As Bert took a step toward him, the boy whirled and raced out the back door.

Yelling, the other children ran after him. He

dashed this way and that, taunting his pursuers.

Finally they made a half circle around him at the end of the swimming pool. As they closed in, Danny hopped onto the diving board.

"Now we've got you!" said Bert. He and Charlie stepped onto the board, cutting off Danny's escape.

"You'll tell where those papers are," said Charlie with a grin, "or you'll walk the plank!"

Danny edged out farther away from them. The other two boys began to jump. As the board bounced up and down Danny struggled to keep his balance.

"Cut it out!" he yelled. "I got my good clothes on!"

But the board bounced higher and Danny flew off. As he landed with a splash, Bert and Charlie toppled off too.

Danny rose and swam to the side. Sputtering angrily, he climbed out and ran off. The other boys got out, dripping and laughing.

"Oh, that was such fun!" exclaimed Susie, clapping her hands. "Danny was so mad!"

"But he didn't tell us where the book stuff is," said Nellie.

"We know he took the things," said Bert. "When he starts thinking about the police, he'll tell."

Half an hour later the boys had dry clothes on and the kitchen had been cleaned up. As the last dish was put away, the children heard the

"You walk the plank, Danny!"

doctor's car come into the driveway. All of them ran to greet him and Mama Luisa.

While the housekeeper went to the kitchen to prepare supper, the children and Joe sat in the doctor's study and reported what had happened while they were away.

"I've called the locksmith," said Joe. "He'll be here tomorrow to fix this door."

The doctor looked worried about the prowler, but laughed when he heard the trick played on Danny. "I'll get the book material," he said, "by telephoning his aunt."

He called Mrs. Rugg and explained. "She will speak to Danny," he reported to the children when he hung up, "and call us back."

While they waited for the telephone to ring, Nan asked if Dr. Funnybone had found out anything about Skipper York.

"Yes. I had a hunch he would be in touch with the Sunken Treasure Club in Miami. I went to see the secretary, who is a friend of mine. He said that Skipper York has been using their library a lot lately. He is especially interested in the Silver Key wreck."

"I wonder if he found out anything," said Nan.

"Probably the same thing I did," the doctor replied.

"What was that?" Flossie asked eagerly.

"I saw a letter there," said the doctor, "from a man who used to go fishing around here years ago. He claimed to have spotted the top part of a wooden statue on the shore of Silver Key. He was in his boat at that time. He wanted to land, but the tide was out and he couldn't take his boat in. When the tide changed, he went back—"

"—and the statue was gone," Bert guessed.

"Right," said the doctor. "Probably the tide washed it away. But it could reappear if it's on the bottom nearby.

"I also found a copy of an old document in which the captain of the *Isabella* listed certain goods he was taking from Spain to Mexico. He mentioned hiding important papers inside a hollow statue head. Perhaps his wife hid the birds there on the return trip."

"Then Skipper Zingo," Bert said, "knows there's a chance the head may turn up again on Silver Key and the birds may be in it."

"We must do some treasure hunting of our own," the doctor decided. "If Zingo gets those silver birds, they'll disappear forever."

"That would be too bad," said Nan. "They should be in a museum where everyone can see them."

Bert meanwhile was casting anxious looks at the telephone on the desk. Mrs. Rugg had not called.

"Danny's leaving on the nine o'clock plane tonight," said Bert unhappily. "I'll bet his aunt can't make him tell."

The doctor glanced at his watch and picked up the telephone. After a while he frowned and said, "No answer."

"Maybe she'll get it out of him on the way," said Teddy.

"If she doesn't call soon, I'll contact his parents in Lakeport," said the doctor. Then looking at the children's worried faces, he said, "How would you all like to call home? You can surprise your mothers and fathers."

The children smiled. "I'd like that," said Susie, " 'cause sometimes I kind of miss my mommy and daddy."

"You can talk to your parents first, Susie," said the doctor, as he started dialing the call.

For the next fifteen minutes the children took turns talking to their homes. Flossie and Freddie sent hugs and kisses to Snoop, the cat, and to the Bobbsey dogs, Snap and Waggo, as well as to Dinah and Sam, who worked for Mr. and Mrs. Bobbsey.

"Oh, that was fun!" said Teddy when the calls were over. "My father said he might not know me when I come home if I'm all suntanned."

Suddenly the telephone rang. Nan raced to answer with the others at her heels.

"Who is it?" asked Bert quickly.

"Wrong number," Nan replied gloomily as she hung up.

"Let's play something," Flossie suggested.

The others agreed. Dr. Funnybone brought out several games and the children played them on the dining room table.

Once Nan looked out the window. "It's raining hard," she said.

About ten o'clock the telephone rang. Everyone dashed to Dr. Funnybone's study. The children watched breathlessly as he picked up the receiver. He listened a moment and smiled.

"All right, thank you," he said and hung up. He turned to the children. "The stories and pictures are in an old trunk under the seat in the gazebo."

"Yeah!" cried Freddie.

The doctor explained that Danny's aunt had made Danny tell the truth just before he boarded the plane.

"He hid the things in his suitcase, but he was afraid his aunt might find them, so he took everything to the gazebo yesterday when we were away."

Freddie wanted to go out and get the papers at once. "No," said the doctor, "it's raining too hard. We'll get them first thing in the morning."

In the middle of the night Nan awoke with a start. She had heard a noise downstairs.

She poked Nellie and explained. "Come on!" she said. "Let's go into the hall and listen."

As the girls stepped out of their room, pulling on their robes, they found Bert leaning over the banister.

"Shh!" he said.

Suddenly there came a whooshing sound and then clicking.

"It's the owl," whispered Nan. "Something scared him. We'd better find him before he hurts himself."

Bert took the green bone flashlight from his robe pocket and they started downstairs.

"Put on the light," said Nellie, "so we can find Mr. Click."

"No!" said Bert sharply. "Come here!"

He was at the back door looking across the yard. The girls joined him. A tall man wearing a cape was coming out of the gazebo with a large box on his shoulder.

CHAPTER XVI

A Risky Trip

"AFTER HIM!" Bert urged, dashing out the kitchen door.

"Nellie, sound the alarm!" cried Nan as she ran after her twin.

As they leaped off the porch, the intruder in the cape went racing down the path. Behind them the iron bell clanged loudly.

The tall prowler made extraordinary speed. He ran in long, easy strides despite the small wooden chest he carried on his shoulder. He reached the dock well ahead of them, jumped into a motorboat and sped out into the bay.

"Missed him!" Bert panted angrily as he stopped beside the dock.

"It's the black motorboat," said Nan, "running without lights." They watched the craft speed toward the island and blend with the darkness.

Bert and Nan hurried up the path. When they reached the back porch, everyone else was there. Nellie was answering their excited questions. Bert reported the prowler's getaway.

"Now the spooks have our stories and pictures," said Flossie sadly. "What'll we do?"

"Go after 'em," Charlie answered.

"I'm for that," Joe agreed. "Okay, doctor?"

"Yes," he said. "You and I and the older children will go at once."

As Mama Luisa took the younger ones back to bed, the others hurriedly dressed.

Five minutes later the detective party arrived at the boathouse.

"Wait!" said Joe. He pointed out into the bay. "That fog is rolling in fast. We can't chance going out in this."

"You're right," the doctor said. "It's too risky. Besides, we could never find the prowlers in this fog."

"It'll probably clear by morning," said Bert. "We can go then." Disappointed, they went back to bed.

Bert awoke at dawn. Hearing a noise in the hall, he peered out of his door. Nan was starting down the stairs.

"Where are you going?" he whispered.

"I can't sleep. I thought I'd get something to eat."

"I'll go with you," he said.

In the kitchen they munched oatmeal cookies

and drank milk. Now and then Bert went to the window to see if the fog had lifted.

"It's still pea soup," he said gloomily.

Suddenly the telephone shrilled. The twins jumped in fright.

"Who would be calling at this hour?" Nan asked.

The phone stopped ringing. "That means the doctor answered it in his room," Bert observed.

A few minutes later they heard his hurried steps on the front stairs. They went out into the hall.

"Hello!" he said, surprised. "What are you doing up?"

Quickly Bert explained. "Is something wrong?" he added.

"Yes," the doctor answered, grabbing his black bag from the table. "That was an emergency call. There was an explosion in a hotel up in the town of Key Largo. Every doctor in the area has been called." He opened the front door and said, "I don't know what time I'll be back. Joe will take you to the island." As he started out the screen door, he turned around and said, "Remember, be careful!"

"We will," Nan promised.

Moments later his motor started and the little car shot down the driveway.

All morning the children waited for the fog to clear. They worked on their stories for a while, but Bert could not concentrate. By early afternoon a chill, damp wind had blown the fog away, but the day was still gray.

"Do we have to go to the island, Joe?" asked Teddy. "I'd rather feed the dolphins."

"So would I," Susie piped up.

"I'll take you, darlings," said Mama Luisa. "I've been wanting to see Cousin Pablo Garcia anyway."

Freddie and Flossie decided to go with Joe and the older children. Taking raincoats and hats, they all headed for the dock.

As they piled into the *Flying Lime,* Joe cast a worried look at the sky. "This is crazy weather," he said. "The radio said there would be no rain, but I don't like the looks of the sky. If it doesn't clear up soon, we'll have to come back. We don't want to get caught in a storm."

As they shot across the water, the spray against their faces was cold and the wind whipped the water into little whitecaps.

"I'm taking no chances on getting stranded," said Joe. "We'll anchor a little distance off-shore and wade to the island."

"Remember to be quiet," Charlie warned. "Sound travels very clearly over water."

Joe cut the motor and dropped anchor. Bert took off his shoes and dropped over the side.

The water came to his knees. He and Charlie started to carry the small twins to the shore.

"Ooh, it's squishy," said Nellie, giving little squeals as they walked toward the beach.

"Will the sea hare bite?"
Flossie asked.

Near the island the water grew shallow and clearer.

"What's that, Joe?" whispered Freddie from Bert's shoulder. He pointed to something in the water among the weeds.

"A sea hare," Joe said. He scooped up a small soft thing shaped like a half moon.

"Is it really a hare?" asked Nan.

"It's a little sea animal," Joe explained.

"May I hold it?" Flossie asked. "Will it bite?" She leaned over from Charlie's shoulder.

"No," Joe replied. "But it does something strange."

Flossie held out one hand and he placed the creature on her palm.

Nellie made a face. "Floss, how can you!"

The next moment the odd animal sent out a beautiful purple fluid.

"Ooh!" cried Flossie and dropped it.

"Shh!" the others warned.

"It won't hurt you," said Joe. "Whenever the sea hare is frightened and wants to hide, it sends out a cloud of that ink and swims away behind it."

When the waders reached shore, they put their shoes on again.

"We must be very quiet," Joe reminded them. He was hoping no one had heard Flossie cry out when she dropped the sea hare.

Single file, with the young twins in the middle, the detectives started into the jungle. As they made their way in the gloom over roots and swampy spots, they stopped now and then to listen.

"I'm sure I heard someone behind us," whispered Nan. They stood still, hardly breathing, but there was no further sound.

Cautiously the searchers moved on. At last they reached the big clearing. It was empty. The children looked around carefully.

Joe's eyes, however, were on the sky. Just then a sharp gust of wind slapped the leaves. Thunder rumbled.

"Come on!" said Joe. "There's no time to lose. We must get back to the boat. If we hurry, we might be able to make the mainland before the storm gets too bad!"

The seven turned back and made their way running and stumbling down the jungle trail.

"But the chest!" Freddie panted. "Our stories and pictures!"

"They'll have to wait," called Joe. "I don't want to be out on the bay when the storm breaks."

"And we don't want to be marooned on this island!" said Nellie.

As they came out on the beach bright pink lightning streaked across the slate gray sky. Thunder boomed. Flossie grabbed Nan's hand.

"Don't stop!" Joe cried. "Into the boat!"

"But our shoes will be soaked," Nellie protested.

"Forget it," Joe shouted. "Go straight to the boat!"

Bert hoisted Flossie to his shoulder, and Freddie climbed to Joe's.

The older children splashed into the water with their shoes on and waded as fast as they could to the boat. Quickly Joe and Bert dropped the young twins into the *Flying Lime* as the others scrambled over the sides. The boat was rolling hard in the waves.

The children grabbed their raincoats from the seats and huddled under them. The motor roared as Joe cut a large half circle to head back toward the mainland.

The next moment the black clouds burst open and rain poured down. The wind slapped the waves against the boat, nearly swamping it.

"Hang on!" Joe cried. But the next moment the boat rose on a huge swell and tipped sideways.

"Help!" the young twins screamed.

"We're turning over!" Charlie yelled.

CHAPTER XVII

Island Discovery

THE CHILDREN SCREAMED and clung to the sides. Desperately Joe twisted the wheel so he could shoot straight through the wave. Spray showered over them.

"We'll never make it home!" Joe shouted. "We'll have to go back!"

His six passengers huddled under their raincoats as the craft headed back for the island. They skirted the beach until Joe spotted an inlet sheltered by overhanging branches. He nosed the *Flying Lime* into the narrow stream and dropped anchor. Everyone stepped ashore in the gloomy jungle.

"It's not raining much in here," said Freddie, looking up. "The branches make a roof."

"That's called a canopy," Joe remarked. A crash of thunder nearly drowned out his words. Flossie grabbed her sister's hand.

"As long as we're stranded here," Nan said, "we may as well explore."

"Let's go to the other side of the island," Charlie suggested. "We've never explored that."

"Maybe the ghost ship is anchored there," Bert remarked.

"Okay," Joe agreed. "We'll follow this inlet to the end. Then if we go to the right we'll hit the path. We take that to the big clearing and from there we'll pick up another trail I know which goes to the far side of the key. Everybody understand?" They all nodded.

"If anybody gets lost," he added, "head for the center of the island. You're almost sure to hit the clearing sooner or later, and the rest of us will wait for you there."

They all slipped into the raincoats and hats they had not had time to put on. With Bert leading, they started along the swampy bank. A few yards ahead, a heavy tangle of vines hung across the stream. As Bert passed beyond it, he stopped in surprise. The black motorboat was anchored there.

"Uh-oh," Freddie whispered. "The spooks are here!"

"Now we've got 'em," said Joe with a grin. "They won't be able to get out past our boat."

"They might use the galleon to get away," Bert remarked, "but they'd never take it out in this weather."

Before going on, the young detectives examined the craft, but found no clues to the owners. At the end of the inlet, Joe took the lead. Walking was hard and the line stretched out with the older twins at the end. Suddenly Nan stumbled and caught herself on a tree trunk.

"You okay?" asked Bert softly.

"Yes, but my foot is stuck." It was wedged under a mangrove root.

Bert grasped his sister's ankle and tried to pull her free. It was no use. "See if you can get out of your shoe," he suggested.

Nan wiggled her foot and managed to slip out of the loafer. Then Bert was able to work it loose.

"Thanks," said Nan, putting the shoe on.

The others were out of sight by this time, and the twins hurried to catch up. After a while Bert stopped.

"I'm not sure of the way," he said.

Nan looked worried. "We could call, I guess, but the spooks might hear us."

"Better not," her twin said. "I think it's this way."

Bert turned to his left. Soon they came to another stream overhung with branches. As they followed it they suddenly saw a light at the end of the green tunnel. Beyond was the gray, wind-whipped water of the bay.

Bert groaned. "We're going in the wrong direction. We'd better—" He stopped as Nan grabbed his arm.

"Look!" she gasped and pointed some distance ahead to a clump of brush beside the water. Sticking out of it was a man's head. He was lying face down.

The twins' hearts pounded with fright. "Hello!" called Bert softly. The figure did not move. Cautiously the children moved closer. Suddenly they both exclaimed at once.

"It's made of wood!" said Nan. "A statue!"

"Maybe it's the hollow one!" Bert exclaimed as they ran over to the object.

Breathless with excitement, the twins pulled out the wooden head. It was larger than life size and had carved curls.

"This is all there is," exclaimed Nan as the twins turned it over. "The head was broken from the body!"

The stern face of the statue looked up at them. Flecks of paint showed that the eyes and beard had been black. The rest was bare, cracked wood.

Bert lifted the head. "It's heavy," he remarked. "Waterlogged." He shook it. "I don't hear anything rattling inside."

Nan examined the neck. "There's no opening down here," she reported.

"We must look at it carefully," said Bert, "but there's no time now. We have to find the others. They're probably waiting for us right now in the clearing."

With Bert carrying the carving, the twins turned inland and began walking in what they hoped was a straight line. Suddenly Nan noticed that the tangled undergrowth was broken by a rough trail.

"Oh, good!" she said. "I think we've hit the path!"

Both children breathed sighs of relief. "Now we're okay," said Bert. "All we have to do is follow this to the clearing."

They went as fast as they could, taking turns carrying the head. It was in Bert's arms as they approached the tree house.

Nan heard a sound and glanced up. Someone was at the top of the ladder!

"Now I've got you, by zingo!" a harsh voice cried. "Hand over that head!"

A small figure leaped down at them. The twins turned and ran. Skipper Zingo hit the ground off balance and fell. He gave a cry of pain as he struck his knee on a root. But a second later, he jumped up and raced after the children.

"Nan!" Bert gasped. "Get off the path! We'll try to lose him."

They plunged into the thick undergrowth. Soon the twins heard their pursuer thrashing along behind them.

"We'll fool him," said Nan. She tore off her

"Now I've got you, by zingo!"
a harsh voice cried.

rain hat and hurled it as far to one side as she could. It caught on a low branch. Then she and Bert ducked under some low, wet brush to hide. The next moment the man's stumbling footsteps came near, stopped, then went off. toward the hat.

Bert grinned and held up his first two fingers in a V for victory sign.

The twins waited in silence for a few minutes, then were about to creep out, when they heard someone coming from the direction of the path. Was it one of the spooks?

The steps came nearer and nearer. They stopped before the twins' hiding place. Somebody was fumbling with the bushes. Suddenly they were jerked apart.

The children froze. Then they gasped in relief. It was Joe!

"Oh, are we glad to see you!" Nan exclaimed.

"And I'm glad to see you!"

Quickly Bert explained about the wooden head and Skipper Zingo. Joe scowled.

"How did you find us?" Nan asked.

"We missed you when we got to the path," Joe replied. "The others went along to the clearing. I cut back looking for you, then I saw the tip of Bert's shoe sticking out of the brush. Come on," he added. "Let's go back to the others."

After Bert got Nan's hat, the three made their

way back to the path and hastened to the clearing. Charlie, Freddie and the girls were huddled at the edge in the shelter of the trees. It was still raining and the wind was blowing hard.

"Oh, we're so glad Joe found you!" cried Flossie and hugged her brother and sister.

"Hush!" Nellie warned. "Remember the spooks."

Nan and Bert quickly told what had happened. The others were excited about the carved head.

"Let's try to open it," Freddie suggested.

"No," said Bert. "Zingo is probably still on the island. He knows we have this, so he'll keep trying to find us."

"What difference does it make?" asked Charlie boldly. "There are seven of us. We'd be more than a match for Zingo."

"He may be armed," Joe said soberly. "Remember he has a reputation for being dangerous. I think we'd better keep on the move. Our first job is to find out what's going on here."

He located the path on the other side of the clearing and they started for the far shore of the key. After a long walk they came out on a narrow strip of sand. The rain had stopped, but the wind still lashed the water.

Single file, the explorers made their way along the curving coast. As they rounded a bend into a deep cove, they stopped short in amazement. Before them rocked the hulk of the Spanish galleon!

"The ghost ship!" Freddie yelled.

Bert frowned. "That's odd. It's small—not much bigger than the caravel."

Joe drew them all back into the jungle. Then he gave a loud whistle. The children peered through the leaves, watching the deck. No one appeared. Joe whistled again. Still no one came.

"I think it's empty," said Bert. "Let's go aboard and look around."

"But the spooks are on the island." Freddie looked frightened. "Suppose they come back and catch us."

"It's our only chance," Bert argued. "Besides they can't be anywhere near, or they would have shown up by now to find out who was whistling."

"All right," Joe said. "We'll move fast."

A rope ladder hung down close to the shore from midship. Joe held the wooden head while Bert got a footing. Then he took the carving and went up. The others followed.

They stood looking around at the deck and the raised castle structure at the bow. The carved decorations had fresh gold paint on them.

"It's not a real galleon," said Bert. "It's too little and not old enough."

"The cabins are below," Nan pointed out.

"Let's examine those first. Maybe we'll find some clue to what this is all about."

They walked over to a low door with a rounded top. Charlie opened it cautiously and they all peered down a narrow stairway into a large cabin.

It was furnished with an old-fashioned desk in one corner, a large chair next to a bunk and a heavy wooden table in the middle. No one was there.

"What funny windows," said Flossie as they filed down the steps. The many-paned glass windows slanted out over the water as the sides of the cabin did.

But the others were eyeing four large lamps on standards and a big metal box in a corner. It was connected to a generator and had a grilled front.

"What's that thing?" Freddie asked.

"Let's find out," said Charlie.

Bert put the head on a chair and walked over to the box. Seeing a red button on the front, Charlie pressed it.

WHOOSH! A terrific wind shot out and hurled the boys backward. Thunder boomed. Joe shielded his head with one arm. Struggling against the howling gale, he managed to switch off the box.

"Whew!" exclaimed Charlie as he and Bert got up from the floor. Nellie's long hair had been blown into tangles.

"A wind machine!" Nan cried. "So the spooks made the storm!"

"And the thunder came from here," Flossie put in excitedly. She held up a box in a leather case. "It's a tape recorder. I found it on the desk. See!" She pressed a button and thunder boomed again.

"But the lights," said Nellie, trying to comb her hair, "what do they use them for?"

"I'm beginning to get an idea," said Nan.

"So am I," her twin declared.

"You mean you know what the spooks are up to?" Freddie asked eagerly.

"What is it?" Charlie demanded.

As Bert opened his mouth to reply, heavy thumps sounded above on the deck. Then footsteps came down the stairs. A voice spoke loudly in Spanish.

Flossie shook with fright. "The spooks!" she whispered. "We're going to be caught!"

CHAPTER XVIII

The Florida Secret

JOE AND THE frightened children looked out the cabin door in the lower deck of the galleon. Heavy boots appeared as a man came down the steps. He was wearing a cape and feathered hat. For a moment the seven were speechless.

Then in chorus they shouted, "Jon!"

"Oh!" he exclaimed, stopping short. Behind him were Gus Wilson, also in Spanish costume, and Jean in a long red dress and a black lace mantilla.

"You're the spooks!" Flossie cried.

"I can't believe it!" Nellie murmured.

"This is a surprise," said Joe quietly.

"What are you up to, anyway?" Charlie asked.

The photographers exchanged looks. "We'll have to tell them, I guess," Jean admitted.

"I think we know." Bert looked at his twin.

Nan nodded. "You're making a movie, aren't you?"

"Yes," Jon answered. "How did you guess?"

"It all fits together," said Nan. "Bright lights for filming at night, a wind machine and tape recorder to make the thunderstorm, and the Spanish costumes."

Bert asked, "You're photographers. If you were filming the picture, how could the three of you also be in it?"

"One person handled the camera when the other two were acting. Sometimes we used a tripod and put the camera on automatic," Jon explained.

"What is your movie about?" Nan asked.

Jean said that when the trio came to Florida they did research in the Sunken Treasure Club library in Miami. There they found the story of the Silver Key wreck.

"We made a screenplay of the legend. For the opening scenes we hired some high school boys from Miami to come down for two days of sailing scenes. The rest of the picture is about only the ship's captain, his wife and the first mate. Jon plays the mate."

"Why didn't you tell us what you were doing?" Freddie asked the trio.

Gus sighed. "Because we're trespassing on Dr. Funnybone's property. We were afraid if he found out he'd make us stop."

"That would have been terrible," said Jean. "We've put so much time and work in it already."

"To say nothing of the small amount of money we had," her brother added.

"I don't think the doctor would make you stop," Nellie remarked. "He's awfully nice."

"But we didn't know that," said Gus. "Besides, we just couldn't afford to take the chance."

Charlie spoke up. "Why didn't you ask him for permission to use the island?"

Jon explained that when they picked Silver Key to work on, they didn't know it belonged to anybody. "We heard that no one had lived in the doctor's house for years. We thought it would do no harm to stage a few scenes in the gazebo."

"We also did one out on the mud flats," put in Gus.

"Imagine how we felt," Jean said, "when we met you on the road and learned the house was now occupied."

"And that the island belonged to the doctor and was going to be used by all of you," her brother added.

"As soon as we left you," Jean continued, "we went home. I put on my costume and picked a hibiscus from behind Gus's trailer. Then the boys drove me to the doctor's house and I sang in the gazebo."

Gus explained, "We wanted you to see a ghost, so you would believe our story and stay away from the island."

"And you chose a hibiscus so we would be sure to connect the singing woman with Silver Key?" Nan suggested.

"Yes," Jean admitted. "We're truly sorry we had to frighten you," she added earnestly. "You know we never would have hurt you."

The three photographers looked very unhappy. "Please believe us," Jon pleaded.

"I do," said Freddie and the others all said they understood. "But why did you take our pictures and stories?" the little boy asked.

"We didn't know they were in the chest, dear," said Jean. She explained that the box was an old Spanish one which they owned.

"It was used for several scenes in the gazebo. We expected to make more so we just left the chest hidden underneath the seat. It seemed a perfectly safe place and saved us having to carry it back and forth."

"It's small," said Gus, "but very heavy."

"After you moved in we kept trying to get it back," said Jon, "but you always turned up at the wrong time."

"Once when Jon and I planned to get it, I was late from a meeting with Skipper Zingo," said Gus. "Later when I came and saw a light, I gave a message to someone I thought was Jon."

"You gave it to Bert and me," said Nan with a smile.

Jon and Gus grinned in spite of themselves and shook their heads. "I knew I'd told the wrong person," said Gus, "when I got back to my trailer and found Jon waiting for me."

"And you faked the thunderstorm that made us leave the island," Charlie broke in. "You sure have a lot of neat equipment. Where did you get this ship?"

"From Skipper Zingo," replied Jon. "He bought the galleon from a little movie company that went broke. He's been keeping it in a cove on a key near here."

"It's not full size," Gus explained. "This is a very simplified model they used mostly for long distance shots."

"The three of us always wanted to make a movie," said Jon. "We hope to enter our picture in film contests so that people will get to know us. Someday, we'd like to have a movie company of our own."

"Oh, I hope we can see the movie sometime," said Flossie eagerly.

"I do, too." Jean looked a little sad. "But now it may not ever be finished."

Just then her brother noticed the head on the chair in the corner.

"Hey!" he exclaimed. "Where did you get *that?*"

Bert explained. "We think maybe this is the head with the silver birds in it," he added, "but we have to find out how to open it."

"Zingo is crazy on the subject of those birds," Gus told the children. "At one time he thought you'd found them."

"Then," said Nan, "it was probably Zingo who searched our house while we were around the grill."

Bert lifted the carving onto the table and everyone gathered around. They examined the head carefully. Where the wooden curls met the forehead, Nan spotted a thin line.

"Here, use this." Joe handed Bert his pocket knife.

Carefully the boy inserted the blade into the crack. At first the swollen wood did not budge, but finally the top of the head came off.

The onlookers scarcely breathed as Nan reached inside and brought out a package wrapped in heavy oilskin. She removed it quickly. Beneath was a canvas covering. Under this, a black velvet wrapping.

"Hurry!" Flossie begged Nan.

Nan placed the parcel on the table and opened it. Two small dark metal pheasants were revealed.

"They're beautiful!" exclaimed Nellie. "See their long, graceful tails!"

"But they don't shine like silver," said Freddie.

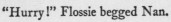
"Hurry!" Flossie begged Nan.

"They will when we clean and polish them," Joe predicted.

"Just see how delicate they are," said Jean. "Every little feather shows. Wouldn't it be wonderful to include them in our movie? That is, if Dr. Funnybone lets us finish it."

"And after that," Bert added, "lots of people will see them in a museum."

"No, they won't!" cried a harsh voice.

The group gasped and looked up. At the top of the stairs stood Skipper Zingo. He had a large yellow can in his hand.

"Our film!" Jean cried.

"Don't make a move," the man warned, "or I'll throw it over the side!"

"Don't you dare!" Gus shouted angrily.

"How did you get that?" Jon started toward him.

Zingo gave an unpleasant smile. "I found it in your storage cabin in the fo'castle. Now hand over the birds," he said, "or you don't get this film back!"

Meanwhile Bert had been quietly edging backward.

"Hurry up!" the skipper snapped. He came down a few steps and held out his hand. "I can't wait all—"

His next words were drowned in the howl of wind. Zingo was blown flat on his back and slid, yelling, down the stairs.

Instantly Gus grabbed the yellow can. Bert

turned off the machine. Joe and Jon jerked Zingo to his feet.

"You think you're smart!" the man panted. "I'll get even! I'll report you to Funnybone! He'll throw you off his property, by zingo!"

"That's enough!"

Everyone looked up in surprise. Dr. Funnybone was hurrying down the steps with three coastguardsmen behind him.

"What's going on here?"

The photographers explained and apologized to the doctor for trespassing on his property.

"You young people have been very kind to the children," said the physician. "I'm perfectly willing to let you finish your movie here. As far as I'm concerned, only one person is trespassing, and that's you, Zingo."

"You want him arrested?" asked one of the coastguardsmen. He was a tall, stern-faced man.

Zingo turned pale.

"No," said the doctor. "But if he ever shows his face here again, I will press charges."

Charlie spoke up. "How did you find us, doctor?"

"When I got home and learned that you children had gone to the island, I was afraid you might be storm-bound, so I called the Coast Guard and came after you. When we didn't find you, I guessed you might have found the galleon and be on it."

"This cove is well hidden," said another of the

coastguardsmen, a young man with straight dark hair. "We didn't spot it right away."

"There's a yellow motorboat in an inlet," said the third. "Whose is that?"

"Mine," Zingo growled.

"Then take it and get off the island," the doctor ordered.

"Everything would have been all right if these nosy kids hadn't interfered," Zingo said bitterly. He turned, ran up the stairs and disappeared.

The doctor thanked the coastguardsmen and told them he would return home in his own boat. After the officers left, Jean hugged Nan and Nellie. Her brothers and Gus thanked Bert and the other children for saving their film.

"Doctor," said Jon, "we certainly appreciate your letting us use the island to finish the film."

The doctor beamed and invited everyone to his house next day. "It will be a party for my eight detectives," he said, smiling.

Meanwhile Bert and Nan gathered up the wooden head and the silver birds. Then Gus took a batch of papers from a leather box on the desk and gave them to Charlie.

"Your book material," he told the children as they prepared to leave.

That evening over a hearty supper, the island adventure was told to Teddy, Susie and Mama Luisa.

"Now we have only one mystery left to solve,"

said Freddie. "What makes Flossie sneeze?"

"I've been working on that since I realized Flossie must have an allergy and not a cold," the doctor replied. "One item after another has been eliminated in my mind. Now I think I finally have the answer. Can anyone guess what it is?"

"The colored mice!" Susie piped up.

"No."

"The water bed!" Charlie announced.

"No."

"Tell us," Nellie pleaded.

"All right. It's Mr. Click," Dr. Funnybone revealed.

"What!" the children chorused.

The doctor grinned. "Every time Flossie sneezed the owl was near her," he stated.

The little girl's face fell. "You mean I'm 'lergic to the owl? I can't play with him?"

"Just don't get too near Mr. Click," Dr. Funnybone advised. "You'll be going home soon and I'm sure your sneezes will stop then."

Next afternoon the Tomsons and Gus arrived with a camera. The children took them out to the patio where a large table had been set with gay paper plates and napkins.

In the center stood the silver birds, now polished and gleaming. Mama Luisa bustled out with Joe, who was carrying a luscious big cake. Dr. Funnybone followed with the owl perched sleepily on his shoulder.

"I have an important announcement to make,"

he said. "Sit down, everyone. In my book I will be able to use every story and every picture you children have made."

"Wow!" yelled Freddie.

"That's super," Bert added, grinning broadly.

The others were excited, too. Nan said, "This makes our vacation perfect. And thanks a million, Dr. Funnybone."

Jon said, "That's great! I'd like to take everybody's picture." He got his camera ready.

"First, the twins and the doctor," Jean directed. "And Flossie, hold your breath."

Flossie sat on Dr. Funnybone's knee and her sister and brothers clustered around him.

"Wake up, Mr. Click," said Flossie. "You're going to have your picture taken." The owl's eyes opened wide.

"Okay," said Jon. "Everyone who thinks Dr. Funnybone is a real great guy say AYE!"

The twins grinned and shouted AYE.

SNAP! went the picture.

Dr. Funnybone smiled. "I think all my little friends are great. Who agrees with me?"

"AYE!" chorused Jon, Jean and Gus.

CLICK! went the owl.